"I am Conor of Tuam, son of Seamus, son of Liam, son of Conor. I am a Knight of the Circle, now in service pledged to Conor I, king of the land which you all once served."

"So?"

Roland's single word spoke volumes. In it was the disdain of royalty for all those beneath it. It implied that the one to whom it was directed was fortunate to be addressed by even a single syllable. And it was a challenge to make one's next utterance worthy of a king's ear or suffer a painful dismissal.

Having in his lifetime served and dealt with all sorts of kings and rulers, Conor was prepared and had his answer ready.

"I come from the waking world, from the kingdom which honors all those in this hall. I come in a time of great trial, a time which threatens to turn that kingdom into a wasteland barren of all life. I come seeking those who are not afraid to fight. I come seeking warriors, I come seeking heroes. Be there any in this hall?"

PADWOLF PUBLISHING BOOKS BY JOHN L. FRENCH

Bianca Jones
Here Be Monsters
Monsters Among Us
The Last Monster
Shadows & Brimstone a Mystic Investigators™ omnibus (Bullets & Brimstone/From The Shdaows) (with Patrick Thomas)
Rites Of Passage: a DMA casefile of Agent Karver and Bianca Jones (with Patrick Thomas)

The Magic Of Simon Tombs

The Matthew Grace Casefiles
Past Sins
Mortal Sins

Agents of the Abyss
Frankenstein: Monsters of the Abyss (with Patrick Thomas)
Detectives of the Abyss: Murder At Castle Dracula (with Patrick Thomas)

The Devil of Harbor City
The Grey Monk: Souls on Fire
The Nightmare Strikes
Bad Cop No Donut (editor)
Mermaids 13 (editor)
Camelot 13 (editor with Patrick Thomas)

OTHER BOOKS BY JOHN L. FRENCH

Bianca Jones: Blood Is the Life
The Last Redhead
When The Moon Shines
Chessie At Bay
The Wages of Syn
The Assassins' Ball (with Patrick Thomas)
The Santa Heist (with Patrick Thomas)
Devilish and Divine (editor with Danielle Ackley-McPhail)
To Hell in a Fast Car (editor)
With Great Power (editor with Greg Schauer)

IN THE RUINS OF CAERLEON

The Chronicles of Conor, Knight of the Circle

JOHN L. FRENCH

PADWOLF PUBLISHING INC.
WWW.PADWOLF.COM
www.facebook.com/Padwolf

IN THE RUINS OF CAERLEON
The Chronicles of Conor, Knight of the Circle
© 2023 John L. French

cover art and design Patrick Thomas

<u>Publication History</u>

All That a Man Could Wish, R. Allen Leider's HELLFIRE LOUNGE 3: JINN RUMMY, Marietta Publishing 2012

The Good, the Bard, and the Ugly, THE SOCIETY FOR THE PRESERVATION OF CJ HENDERSON, eSpec Books 2015 (under the title "What Tales he Knows")

Heir to the Kingdom, Pulp Fiction Stories 60, May 2000, Fading Shadows Publications

Local Catch, MERMAIDS 13: TAILS OF THE SEA, Padwolf Publishing 2012

Only the Dead, ZOMBIES IN TIME AND SPACE, Wildcat Books 2010

Reflected Magic, Alfred Hitchcock's Mystery Magazine, November 2000

Also read *The Reluctant Lady*, in CAMELOT 13, Padwolf Publishing 2018 (written with Susanne Wolf)

Note: The names of the knights Bors the Younger, Marrok the Wolf, Bedivere, Dagonet the Jester, Sagamore the Hothead, Bertilak the Green, and Galahad the Pure, as used in the story "In the Ruins of Caerleon," are copyright Patrick Thomas and are used with his permission.

ISBN 978-1-958310-05-2
First Printing.

Contents

Author's note:

The Conor stories were written over a long period of time, most of them for magazines or anthologies. "Heir to the Kingdom" was the first one written. While it takes place later in Conor's career (after "To Save the Land") I think it's a good place to start. I hope you enjoy the stories. And now:

ONCE UPON A TIME …

HEIR TO THE KINGDOM

In the kingdom of Vilania, there lived a king and a queen. Now at the time of this story, Vilania was at peace, almost everyone had enough food to eat, and there were no ogres, dragons, or giants threatening the land. There was the usual discontent among the peasants, but they had always been unhappy, and always would be, and nobody who counted cared too much about them anyway.

Still, King William and Queen Anne had a problem. They were childless. They had been married for ten years and there was no heir to the throne, no prince to become king when William had finished his reign and went to join his ancestors. There was not even a princess who could be married to an eligible noble of another kingdom and thus ensure a peaceful and uncontested succession.

Desperate for a child, the king and queen consulted the wise men of the court. None of them could help. One did suggest that where wisdom had failed, perhaps magic could succeed. Over the objections of the Prime Minister, who did not like magic and did not trust those who practiced it, the king and queen set out to find a miracle.

They went first to the Old Woman of the Woods. After she had let them in and had given them tea and something to eat, the king placed a gold coin on the table in front of her. Now in this place and at this time, a gold coin placed in front of a witch, wizard, or other worker of wonders compelled an honest answer to any three questions.

The Old Woman put away her teapot, sat down in front of the king, and said, "Ask your questions, Your Majesties, but ask carefully. For the answer is ofttimes only as good as the question, and what is found is not what was sought."

The king spoke first. "Her Majesty and I have long wished for a child, an heir to the kingdom. Will we ever have one?"

Before she spoke, the Old Woman took the teacups from in front of the royal couple. She looked at the leaves left in the bottoms of the cups. She reclaimed her teapot and poured a small amount of cold tea into each cup.

"Drink this," she said to both of them, "then stir the dregs with your left forefinger."

The king and queen did as they were told, and handed their cups back to the Old Woman, who carefully inspected the inside of the cups.

"Neither of you will have a child, but an heir you both will have."

"And just what does that mean?" the queen asked too quickly.

"The meaning is clear, or will become so." The answer was honest, but not helpful.

"What are we to do?" the king asked, forgetting the ways of prophecy and hoping for some direct advice.

"What you will, for your good and that of the kingdom." With that, the Old Woman picked up the gold coin that was her payment and would speak no more.

With a word of farewell, the king and queen left her.

Confused and disappointed, King William and Queen Anne went to see the Wizard of the Tower. Again, after tea and something to eat, they laid a gold coin in front of him, compelling him to answer their questions honestly.

"Ask your questions," the Wizard said, "And I will answer as I am asked."

On their way to the Wizard's tower, the king and queen had argued over which questions to ask, and how to ask them. Once that had been settled, they agreed that only the king would speak.

"Wizard," asked the king, "Will the queen and I have any children?"

The Wizard looked into the eyes of the king and queen, then at their palms. Then, as carefully as the king had asked, so the wizard answered. "You will not sir," the Wizard smiled at his wordplay, "nor will the queen bear a child, yet a child you both shall have."

"And this child shall be heir and prince?"

"He shall." The Wizard made a slight bow to the king, to acknowledge his skill in asking two questions in one.

"And how is this to be, if the queen and I are not to have children of our own?"

The Wizard smiled and picked up his coin. "In your question,

Your Majesty, was your answer." And he would speak no more.

With a word of farewell, the king and queen left him.

Still confused, but with some hope, the king and queen went to see the Old Man in the Mountain. After traveling a day, a night, and another day, they came to the cave in which the Old Man lived. He did not offer them tea, or anything to eat. He did not even let them into his cave. Instead, he had them stand outside, while he spoke from the darkness.

"I know why you've come. Throw in the coin and ask your questions."

This time it was agreed that the queen would do the asking. Before she did, she told the Old Man what the others had said.

"I care not for the words of others," said the Old Man. "You have questions or you do not. Ask or be gone from here."

"Do you know what the others meant?"

"I do," answered the Old Man.

"Then what did the words of the Old Woman mean?"

And he told her.

"And what did the words of the Wizard mean?"

And he told her and suddenly all was clear, and the king and queen knew what they would have to do to have a child.

When they returned to their castle, the king announced that the queen was going away for a time, to stay with her mother in a neighboring kingdom. Everyone in the court rejoiced at this news, for they thought they knew what this meant. They had been waiting for this, and ten years is a long time to wait.

After the queen had left, the king summoned the captain of his guard.

"Find me a man. I need someone clever, someone who knows how to keep his mouth shut, a soldier who will follow his king's orders without question. Find me a man like this, but one whom no one will miss, and whom you can do without."

The captain of the guard found such a man and sent him to the king.

"You are to search the kingdom," the king told the man, "and find me a special couple. They should resemble the queen and me. Find me such a couple, but only if the wife is with child. Do not search among the nobility or the upper classes of merchants. I do not want you to have anything to do with those who are normally at court. Look instead among the townsfolk and farmers."

"And what does His Majesty wish me to do when I find such a couple?"

"Wait until the child has been born. If the child is a girl, find another couple. If the child is a boy, take him to the queen."

"How long have I to accomplish this?"

"No more than nine months."

"And what of the parents?" the soldier asked, his hand on his sword so that the king would know what he was asking.

"Let them live if possible. If they are killed, questions may be asked. Leave a doll or something in the boy's place. Then the fairies will be blamed for stealing the child, and the doll burned as a changeling. That will be the end of it."

And so it was done. A child was stolen and delivered to the queen. Smiling, the queen looked down at the child, who was lying in the basket the soldier had used as a cradle. Her smile faded and she turned to the soldier with a look of puzzlement and disappointment.

"It is a small thing, and will not be noticed when he is properly dressed." The soldier explained. "Other than that, he looks as if he could be the king's own son."

"He is the king's son," Queen Anne said quickly, accepting the child. She gave orders that the new prince be dressed in the manner befitting the heir to the throne. To the soldier, she gave a bag of gold and another of silver.

"The gold is the reward for your service and your silence. The silver is for you to travel as far from this land as the coins in the bag will take you. If you ever return, all you will find waiting for you is a sword in the dark and an unmarked grave."

The soldier bowed, left his queen, and was never seen again.

The queen returned from her mother's kingdom with a son she called her own, and the Kingdom of Vilania had a prince and an heir.

Several days before the queen was presented with her new child, a farmer's wife gave birth to a beautiful baby boy. That he was his father's son there was no doubt, and both his parents loved him from the moment they first laid eyes on him.

A month after the boy was born, the farmer woke early. He would check on his new son, and if he were still asleep, would go out to tend to his animals. His wife he would let sleep. Once the animals had been fed and the cows milked, he would come back inside his cottage to wake her and bring her the baby.

Wake his wife he did, but not in the manner he had intended. When he checked on his son, the cradle was empty. His cry of anguish woke his wife and startled the animals. As she hurried from her bed, she called out to him, asking what the trouble was. He cried, "The boy is gone," and rushed outside to try to find some trace of his child.

His wife followed him out. She watched as he walked around the cabin, looking for a sign. At the cottage window, there was a tuft of wolf's fur.

"Karl, look."

"I saw it, Helen, but there are no tracks. And the ones I made last night before turning in are gone too. Someone has wiped them away, and wolves do not do that. Our boy has been stolen."

Leaving Helen to search the farm for some sign of the boy, Karl went to rouse the village. The villagers all met back at the farm, and they searched as far as they dared, even some distance into the woods. They found nothing.

As evening came on, the villagers, defeated in their search, gathered in the couple's small cottage.

"It was the fairies," said one old man. "They've stolen children before."

"No," said another, "It was a wolf, Karl found his fur."

"Wolves do not wipe their tracks away," said a younger man, who, being young, did not believe in child-stealing wolves or fairies.

"There is one kind of wolf that will, and he does not always need the moon to change."

"It could still be a man," said the young man.

"Who then?" asked Karl. "Who was it who stole my child? Was it one of you?"

Karl looked around the room, staring into each of their faces, finding no guilt, seeing no one turn away.

"No, I cannot, will not believe that of my neighbors and friends. And it has been months since the last stranger came through here."

"The soldier," someone reminded him. "He stayed at the inn only one night. He was a friendly sort, bought drinks, and talked into the early hours."

"So it was none of us, and it could be no one else." Karl picked up the tuft of fur someone had laid on the table.

"This is beyond what we can do," he said. "We need help."

So the villagers took what money they could spare, and changed it for three gold coins. And Karl and Helen set out to find a miracle.

They went first to the Old Woman of the Woods. After she had let them in and had given them tea and something to eat, Karl placed a gold coin on the table in front of her.

The Old Woman put away her teapot, sat down in front of the couple, and said, "Ask your questions but ask carefully. For the answer is ofttimes only as good as the question, and what is found is not what was sought."

"Where is our child?" asked Helen, hoping that the question was simple enough for a simple answer.

For a while, the Old Woman did nothing. She just sat and stared at the farmer and his wife. If her eyes glistened and she blinked away a tear, Karl and Helen did not notice. "I cannot say," she finally answered, as honest a reply as she could make.

"Will we ever find him?" Karl asked the second question.

This time, the Old Woman took the teacups from in front of the couple. She looked at the leaves left in the bottoms of the cups. She reclaimed her teapot and poured a small amount of cold tea into each cup. "Drink this," she said to both of them, "then stir the dregs with your left forefinger."

Karl and Helen did as they were told, and handed their cups back to the Old Woman, who carefully inspected the inside of the cups.

"Neither of you will find him," came the answer. The Old Woman, constrained by the asking, phrased her answer as best she could.

"Is he safe?" Helen's concern for her son, so little and so helpless, outweighed all other matters, and so she wasted her last question.

"He is safe." With that, the Old Woman picked up the gold coin that was her payment and would speak no more.

Disappointed, Karl and Helen went to see the Wizard of the Tower. Again, after tea and something to eat, they laid a gold coin in front of him.

"Ask your questions," the Wizard said, "And I will answer as I am asked."

"Where is our son?" Karl asked, hoping that the Wizard could answer what the Old Woman could not.

The Wizard was silent for a time. If the couple noticed that his hands gripped the edge of the table and his knuckles whitened, they did not think it important.

"I cannot say" was the honest answer.

Karl had expected this answer, and so had prepared his next question carefully.

"How can he be found?"

The Wizard looked into their eyes, then at their palms. Then, as carefully as Karl had asked, the wizard answered. "He can be found only if the right person looks for him."

Karl, worried that Helen would again ask after the boy, quickly asked his last question. "And who is this person?"

"A hero." And the Wizard would speak no more.

Still worried, but with some hope, Karl and Helen went to see the Old Man in the Mountain. After traveling a day, a night, and another day, they came to the cave in which the Old Man lived. He did not offer them tea, or anything to eat. He did not even let them into his cave. Instead, he had them stand outside while he spoke from the darkness.

"Keep your money. I have nothing to say, no answers to your questions."

Nevertheless, Karl threw in the gold coin.

"I have but one question to ask, Old Man. Where can we find a hero?"

The Old Man told them and they returned home.

Karl and Helen returned to their cottage just long enough to rest from the journey. Then they set out again. They traveled to a village on the other side of the kingdom. There they found a man everyone said had once been a hero.

His name was Conor. It was said of him that before he had come to live in this place, he had rescued a princess and saved her kingdom.

Before that, he had slain a dragon and taken its treasure for his own. And before that, he fought a giant, defeated him, then befriended him.

Conor was supposed to have married the princess and was to rule her kingdom after her father died. But his princess fell in love with his friend, the giant, and the two ran off, taking much of the dragon's gold with them. Heartbroken, Conor left the kingdom, taking with him the rest of his treasure. After much wandering, he settled in the village where Karl and Helen found him.

Conor received the couple graciously. He invited them to sit and offered them food and drink. While they ate, Karl looked around Conor's house.

The house they had come to in search of a hero was no bigger than their cottage back at the farm. The furnishings were richer, however, as befits a man who still has some part of a dragon's hoard to call his own. There were weapons all about. There was a sword in a leather scabbard hanging on a hook. A mace was leaning against a chair near the door, and a dagger lay on a table between the bed and the far wall.

Karl then studied Conor. He was only slightly taller than Karl, and not as heavily muscled as the heroes in the songs the troubadours sang. But the muscles were there, and they were of the type one gets by swinging swords and holding shields, and not by pushing plows and digging crops. The man he had hoped to be a hero at least looked the part.

Conor caught Karl studying him. "Satisfied?" asked the larger man.

"I will be after you hear our tale, and say yes to our plea."

Dinner was over, so Conor cleared the dishes and invited the couple to tell their story. He listened without a word as Karl and Helen alternated telling him about finding their son gone, their search for him, and their journey to the three seers.

When they had finished, Conor thought for a while, and then said, "It is odd that none of the Three could tell you of your son. Usually, what one does not know, another does."

"Could it be the fairies?" asked Helen. "Is that why they could not say where our son is? Could fairy magic be keeping them from seeing him?"

"It is possible," allowed Conor. "But let us look for the boy in this world before traveling to the next. I have been to Faerie before. It is easier to get there than to leave it. Let that be the last thing we try."

"Then you will help us?" The couple at last had some hope.

"I will try, as best I can."

Karl paused, the next matter being the most difficult. "Sir, we are simple farm folk. We do not have much, but what we have is yours if you find our son. Our farm will be yours, and we will work it for you, if only you return him to us."

Conor smiled and nodded to acknowledge the farmer's offer. "I thank you, sir, but your farm is yours, and will remain so. Let us worry about finding the boy, and then discuss other matters."

Karl was satisfied. He had found his hero.

Conor questioned the couple about all that had occurred, from their discovery of the boy's disappearance to the exact words said to them by the Three, and all else that was said and done. When he had finished and had learned as much as he could from the pair, he sent them home, promising to come to their village as soon as he had some news, be it good or ill.

As Karl rose to leave, he moved stiffly and walked to the door as if in some pain. Something made Conor ask about it.

"Friend Karl, I could not help but notice your walk. Are you injured in some manner? You and your wife are free to spend the night if you like."

Karl thanked Conor for his concern. "It's nothing, it is just that we have been walking much over this last week, and my feet hurt." The farmer smiled. "My shoes are too tight. They have always been too tight and always will be.

"Many years ago my great-grandfather was a traveling man. One day he stopped in a Romany camp, and his horse, not being properly tied, got loose and trod on the foot of an old woman. She, of course, put a curse on my great-grandfather. Ever since then, the shoes of all the men in our family have been too tight."

Despite Conor's repeated offers, the pair would not rest with him overnight. Instead, they set out for their own village.

There were many reasons why someone would steal a baby. Most were unpleasant to think about. Sacrifice? Most of those stories were told only to discredit one religion or the other. Slavery? Slavers would take children able to fend for themselves and not burden themselves with an infant that had to be cared for. The fairies would steal a human child and raise it as their own, so weak were their bloodlines that too few fairy children were being born. If that was the case, the child was lost. Time ran differently in the Land of Youth. Conor himself had lost a year by spending just a week there. By the time the boy was found and rescued, he'd be a full-grown man.

Still, one did not have to be a fairy to be unable to have children. He knew of a few childless couples who would have eagerly accepted a foundling who may have not been honestly orphaned. Desperate people do desperate things.

Conor then thought then of what Karl and Helen had said about the soldier. He, too, remembered a soldier who had passed through his village. This soldier had only spent one night and had bought drinks for all. Conor had spent some time with him, trading stories of wars and adventures. Conor also remembered that the soldier had asked about village life, of weddings and funerals, of births and deaths. Conor had paid no attention to it then, had thought it just the questions of a man too long from his own home. Now, with a child gone, Conor wondered why this soldier of the king had been so interested.

A soldier of the king, Conor thought, *a king whose queen had just been delivered of a son after a great many childless years.*

With this now worrying him, Conor set out, knowing that miracles were hard to come by, and very often, a man had to make his own.

He went first to the Old Woman of the Woods. After she had let him in and had given him tea and something to eat, Conor placed a gold coin on the table in front of her.

The Old Woman put away her teapot, sat down in front of him, and said, "Ask your questions but ask carefully. For the answer is ofttimes only as good as the question, and what is found is not what was sought."

Now Conor was wise in the ways of sorcerers and witches and knew that truth and honesty were not always the same. They were at best close friends, who often traveled together, but sometimes went their own ways. He knew how to ask questions.

"A farmer and his wife came to you to ask after their lost child. Where is the child?"

"I cannot say," answered the Old Woman honestly.

"And why," Conor asked, "can you not say?"

"Because," she said with a smile, "Someone with the power to command me has forbidden me to."

"And who is this someone?"

"The king." With that, the Old Woman picked up the gold coin that was her payment and would speak no more.

Satisfied, Conor went to see the Wizard of the Tower. Again, after tea and something to eat, he laid a gold coin in front of him, compelling him to answer his questions honestly.

"Ask your questions," the Wizard said, "And I will answer as I am asked."

"A farmer and his wife came to you to ask after their lost child. Where is the child?"

"I cannot say," answered the Wizard honestly.

"And why," Conor asked, "can you not say?"

"Because," the Wizard said, having hoped this question would come, "Someone with the power to command me has forbidden me to."

"And who is this someone?"

"The queen." With that, the Wizard would speak no more.

Conor next went to see the Old Man in the Mountain. After traveling a day, a night, and another day, he came to the cave in which the Old Man lived. The Old Man did not offer him tea, or anything to eat. He did not even want to let him into his cave. Instead, he told Conor to stand outside, and he would speak from the darkness.

"Old Man," Conor called into the cave, "I did not travel a day and a night and another day just to yell into the dark. You will invite me to enter, or I will come in anyway and drag you out into the sun. I've always wondered what the daylight would do to bones as old as yours, and now is a good time to find out."

"Is that you, Conor?"

"It is, Rumpel. I've come about the boy."

"I thought you would, that's why I sent them to you. Come in.

We must talk."

Conor walked into the darkness of the cave. Holding out his hands to keep from walking into walls, he felt his way past first one turn, and then another. He finally came to a chamber brightly lit by torches.

After they had eaten, Conor asked the Old Man, "Why tell the king and queen to steal a child and then send for me to rescue it?"

"It would have occurred to William and Anne eventually. The Wizard, the Old Woman, and I only told them what we knew would happen, what they had to do if the kingdom was to avoid some messy battles when the king finally died."

"They could have fostered a child and raised him as their own." Conor shook his head at the Old Man. "Why did you not tell them that?"

"They did not ask me what to do, only what the others had meant."

"So now, Old Man, I must break into the palace, steal the prince, and return him to his rightful parents."

"If that's a question, Conor, it's your third one, and you owe me a gold coin. No, that is what you must not do. For if you do, then the kingdom will again be without an heir, and we will again face civil war. Either that or the king and queen will steal another child."

Conor sat silently, weighing the good of a kingdom against the anguish of two parents. He knew what he would have done, had he married his princess and were now a king.

"A kingdom, a king, must serve the people, not the other way. They are not fit to rule, Rumpel, those who would steal our children."

"Agreed, Conor, but what will you do? If you displace William and Anne, who will rule? What is best—a king without an heir or an heir without parents? And are you even sure that the farmers' lost son is the newly born prince?"

"That's three questions from you, Old Man, and now you owe me a gold coin. As for what is best, it is having the boy with his rightful parents, an heir to the throne, and a king and queen who are fit to rule. And as for whether the prince was born on a farm or in a great hall, I believe the answer to that is with a Romany curse. There is only one question left."

Conor got up and brought the teapot back to the table. He poured a small amount of cold tea into his cup. He drank the tea and stirred the dregs with his left forefinger. He passed the cup to Rumpel.

"Read the leaves, Old Man, then look into my eyes and read my palm. I have a question to ask, and then we will each owe the other a coin and will be quits."

And Conor asked his question, and the Old Man was surprised and delighted at both it and the answer.

From the Old Man, Conor purchased two spells. On his way to the capital, Conor stopped at the Tower. From the Wizard he purchased a cloak. He then stopped in the Woods. From the Old Woman he purchased a potion. He then stopped at the village of Karl and Helen and asked Karl to take off his shoes. It was as he had expected.

Conor told the couple part of his plan, and the three of them set off to make a miracle.

It was late when Karl, Helen, and Conor rode into the capital. They took rooms at an inn close to the castle. Helen protested that the inn was far too lavish and much too expensive for them, but Conor insisted, saying that the nearness to the castle more than made up for the cost.

"Besides," he told them, "What is gold for if not to spend?"

They rested until the next afternoon. Conor then took them to the castle, acting the part of a guide, the city dweller showing the country cousins the sights. They passed over the bridge and through the gates, into that part of the castle that was open to all. Though it was a warm day, Conor had the Wizard's cloak over his arm. The potion from the Old Woman was in a flask at his hip. The spells he had committed to memory.

Once in the castle, Conor looked for a secluded spot. He found an alcove under a flight of stairs. Seeing that no one was watching, he told took Karl and Helen aside.

"I'll be leaving you for a while. Stay here and play country bumpkins. 'Ooh' and 'Ah' and ask the guard silly questions. I'll be back soon with good news or bad."

Conor quickly ducked into the alcove and slipped on the cloak.

Karl and Helen watched as all but his head faded from view. Conor gave a Cheshire smile, then threw the hood over his head. He disappeared entirely.

For Conor, the castle lost all of its color. The bold tapestries on the walls were now simple black and white, and the guards' colorful uniforms shades of gray. Unseen, he made his way quietly up the stairs. He looked around until he found the most heavily guarded door. That would be the way into the royal family's private quarters.

He had to wait until someone opened the door to slip in. After that, it was just a matter of finding the nursery. A baby's cry led him there.

Conor watched as anxious nurses fussed over a cradle until the crying stopped. Once the child was quiet, they left him and went back to gossiping in the corner.

Still cloaked, Conor quietly walked over to the cradle. As he bent down over it, the boy looked up at him, smiled, and cooed. Conor wondered if the child in its total innocence could see through the magic, and if so, what he saw.

Very carefully, so as not to startle the child and make it cry out, Conor removed its stockings. Once they were off, Conor looked down at the infant's bare feet. Just as he had hoped and expected, the boy had six toes on each foot, just like his father, and his father before that, and so on. Little did that old Romany woman know that one day her curse would become a blessing.

Not wishing to press his so far remarkable luck, Conor left the stockings off the child and made his way out of the royal quarters and back down the stairs. Let the nurses make of the boy's bare feet what they will.

Conor rejoined Karl and Helen and threw off the cloak. His sudden reappearance startled Karl and he gave out a cry. A couple of guards looked his way but Conor gave a wave to indicate that everything was all right and they turned away.

"He's up there," Conor told the pair. He had to grab Helen to keep her from rushing up to claim the boy.

"No, that's not the way." He looked at the two of them and hesitated. He was about to change their lives forever.

"Listen to me," he whispered, "This will have to be quick. The guards could decide to turn their attentions to us at any moment." He casually looked around. They were still being ignored.

"Karl, you told me that you would pay any price to get your son back. Is that still true?"

"Of course it is."

"Helen, what about you?"

"Yes, anything."

Conor took the flask with the potion out of his pocket. "Then drink this, both of you, and whatever happens, ask no questions until it is all over. And may you both forgive me."

Karl drank first, downing half the liquid. Helen went next, draining the flask. As they drank, Conor began to speak the first of his spells.

Conor stood back as the potion took effect. There was a shimmering, and he watched as the farm couple began to change. Both got older, and Karl grew and gained pounds. His hair changed from a muddy brown to black. His calluses faded and his hands grew smooth.

Helen also changed. Her features grew softer, the lines on her face fading away. She lost pounds, and her dusty blond hair turned golden.

As the couple changed, so did their clothing. Their country clothing became regal finery, adorned with lace and satin.

Somewhere in the palace, Conor's spell should be taking effect. As Karl and Helen changed, so should William and Anne.

Karl and Helen looked at each other in terror, then looked back at Conor. "What is this?" asked Karl, in a voice that did not seem to be his own.

"This is the price—Your Majesty." Helen gasped, realizing what Conor had done.

The attention of the guards was finally on them. Two of them came rushing over only to stop as they saw the couple. They bowed low.

"Forgive us, Your Majesties, we did not see you come down the stairs."

Karl was still speechless. Helen answered, "There is nothing to forgive. You were guarding the entrance, as is your job. The king and I were about to take a walk, but perhaps we should return to the royal suite."

There was a commotion above them. Guards were bringing a couple down the stairs. They looked very much like Karl and Helen's former selves. Neither was being treated very gently.

"But I am the king, I tell you."

"Quiet you, I've told you before, I don't care who you think you are, we've a place for the likes of you."

The sergeant of the guard stopped when he saw what he perceived as the true royal couple. He gave a bow that was remarkably low considering his great size and weight.

Conor spoke his second spell.

"I'm sorry," said the man who looked like Karl. He spoke as in a dream, the words forced out of him. "It was … all a jest that got out of hand." He looked over towards the couple he now saw as the king and queen. "Forgive us."

Karl, now King William, was only now beginning to understand the price he had paid for his son's return. Still, it was Helen, now Queen Anne, who addressed the sergeant.

"Let them go, Sergeant. See them safely back to their inn, and then out of the city." To her old self she said, "You do remember where your inn and your home are, don't you?"

"Yes, I think so," said Queen Anne, now Helen. She looked puzzled for a moment, then named the inn where the three had stayed, and the village where Karl and Helen lived.

"Then take them away, Sergeant, and thank you."

Later that night in the royal chambers, with the new King William and Queen Anne reunited with their child, Conor explained.

"It would have been cruel to leave them with their memories of their old life. Better for them to think it a dream."

"But why, Conor, why all of this?" William waved his arms at the lavish furnishings, but Conor knew his true meaning.

"The problem was, Your Majesty, and you'd best get used to hearing that, was that if I returned your son, those who stole him would only take another couple's child. Either that, or when the king died, there would have been confusion at best, and civil war at worse, over the succession. What was needed was a way to reunite your family yet leave the kingdom with an heir, decent people to raise him, and a good king and queen."

"And how do you know we will make a good king and queen?"

Conor smiled. "I asked the Old Man. He said that you would do no worse, and probably better than those who would steal children."

And so it ended. Karl and Helen, once rulers of a kingdom, returned to their village after their barely remembered trip to the capital. If they behaved strangely after that, their neighbors attributed it to the loss of their son. A year later, they fostered a child from a family with far too many mouths to feed. They lived almost but not quite happily ever after, for there was always a sense that they had lost something special, and belonged somewhere else.

The new king and queen ruled with wisdom and justice, and when they passed on, the kingdom was a much better place for their having ruled it. The new king, Conor I (named after a friend of the family), was much loved by his people and lived a long and happy life.

All That a Man Could Wish

Conor of Scotia was not yet a hero. One day he would be. One day he would usurp a king and place another on his throne so deftly that no one would notice. And one day he would die a hero's death. But those days were yet to be.

This tale takes place when Conor was still a young man looking for adventure. Newly arrived on the continent from his native isle, he was a sword for hire, if the cause was just and the price was right. Sometimes he fought solely for a cause, refusing gold from those who could not pay. Other times, when his purse was thin and his stomach empty … well, he was young and as was said, he was not yet a hero.

Conor had been in service to a baron, charged with guarding his master's keep and those who resided therein. In the naiveté of youth, he foolishly believed this meant that he should protect *all* those who lived within the castle walls. So when he came across a minstrel attacking a serving wench, he did that which he thought right and proper, which was to give the minstrel a sound thrashing, throw the scoundrel in the dungeon, and report to the baron. At the time he had no idea that the minstrel was the baron's cousin. Later, after he had fought his way clear of the keep and escaped on a horse of much better quality than the one on which he had arrived, Conor reflected on his actions. Had he known who the minstrel was, he would still have rescued the wench, but with less thrashing, no head banging into stone walls, and his report would have been of finding the baron's cousin unconscious on the floor.

Wanting to put as much distance between himself and the barony as possible, Conor rode east, crossing into the lands of the Middle Kingdom where a young knight with a sword and a horse could not fail to find a way to fill both his purse and his stomach.

Save that the realm in which Conor found himself had no need of men-at-arms, or so he was told at the Inn of the Full Moon.

"The Duke has an army," the innkeeper assured him, "but it's a small one, mainly for keeping his peace."

Knowing the ways of the world, Conor could not help but ask, "Then how does he keep out raiders and repel invading armies?"

The innkeeper shrugged. "Don't know. Don't care. Hasn't been any trouble like that since Rayford came back from the far eastern lands two decades past."

"As I remember it," said an old man who had emerged from the shadows of a corner table with an empty mug in his hand, "it was Rayford who last caused trouble." The mug hit the bar with a hollow thump as the old man looked at Conor expectantly.

"Saddest sound in the world," Conor said. He nodded at the innkeeper who filled the man's tankard with a not very promising ale. "You were saying, grandfather."

"I was saying that it was just about twenty years ago. Things weren't good like they are now. The old duke let his men do what they pleased and take what they wanted. Taxed the hell out of us too. Then Rayford came in from some place called Baghdad with a foreign-looking young man. It wasn't long after that that there was some commotion up at the castle. The next thing we all knew the old duke was gone and Rayford was running things. Not only that, but he'd married the old duke's youngest sister to make it all legal-like. And that's the last we've had of any troubles around these parts."

"And for twenty years there's been peace? No wars, no plots against the duchy, nothing like that?"

Both the innkeeper and old man shook their heads. "There's always talk or rumors of war and fighting. But it's always someplace else, never here. Now, young sir, will you be needing a bed the night, or will you be moving on."

"Well," Conor said to the innkeeper, "with no work for an honest swordsman, I'll be moving on. Thank you both." He dropped some coins on the counter and left the inn.

Conor had planned to move on, to find a realm in which to ply his trade. He was halfway out of the duchy when the thought came to him that he would very much like to meet this duke who had no need of an army. Yes, he decided, at the least, he should pay his respects to the ruler of the land through which he passed. It was the right and proper thing for a knight such as he to do. Just as it would be the right and proper thing for the duke to offer him a meal and a night's lodging.

Never had Conor seen a castle more unprotected. True, there was the usual two longbow shots distance from the walls to the tree line, and there was a moat and a gate. But the drawbridge was down, the gate stood open and there was only one man on the battlement. Conor approached the castle without encountering any patrols, nor did anyone challenge him as he, an armed knight, rode toward the gate.

No shouts of "Rider approaching" greeted him. Rather, the lone watchmen called out "He's here!" to someone below, a cry that Conor heard repeated several times as he passed the gates into the outer ward. As was courtesy, he dismounted and walked his steed through to the inner bailey.

No archers on the walls ready to cut him down. No swordsmen at the ready should Conor rush the duke's quarters. Only a young man with skin darker than Conor had ever seen awaited him on the grounds.

"Welcome, Sir Knight," the youth said in an accented tongue. "How are you called?"

Conor reasoned that this was the one of whom the old man at the Inn spoke, the one who had returned from Baghdad with Rayford. *He was young then*, Conor thought, *and is young still.* That fact, the cry of "He's here!" and the absence of any visible defense told the knight much.

Sensing that the man before him was a servant of the duke—high placed, well respected, greatly valued, but a servant nonetheless—Conor offered no bow as he introduced himself.

"I am Conor of Tuam, a knight of Scotia, son of Seamus, son of Liam, son of Conor. And how are you called, Sir Mage?"

Excepting the quick smile that crossed his face, the dark young man showed no surprise at Conor's question. "Call me Ismael, Sir Conor. And if you would follow me, the duke awaits you. Your horse will be well attended."

"You were awaiting me?" Conor asked as the two walked toward the inner keep.

"We were awaiting someone. It happened to be you."

"How is that so?"

"You have already answered that question, Sir Conor."

"You are a magician. You caused it to happen."

Another smile appeared on the young mage's face, this one wider and lasting longer. "I am magic itself. And you are here because the duke wished it."

The bards of Scotia had spoken of wishes, Conor recalled as they made their way silently toward the duke; wishes granted by the Fae, the cost of which was always greater than that which was obtained.

There was nothing special about Duke Rayford, not to Conor. He was not overly tall or strong. His looks were not such as to make men follow him or women fall before him. Possibly he was smart or clever. If so, it did not show on his face. Take him off his throne and he could be any man in any village. To the Scotian knight, Rayford was just one of many men who had won his place through strength of wit, force of arms or, perhaps, thinking of the dark, young mage who stood beside the Duke, something more arcane and sinister. Still, Conor addressed the man respectfully, mindful of the courtesies due one's host as well as his hopes that Rayford may have a task that would put gold in his purse.

"You wished to see me, My Lord."

Rayford's left eyebrow rose just a bit at Conor's choice of words. Maybe at a different time he would have laughed, but there was a sadness on his face that said he had not laughed in several days.

"So I did, Sir Knight. Trouble has fallen on my house. My daughter Constance is missing and I wish you to find her." As to make his meaning clear, Rayford looked from Conor to Ismael then back to the knight.

Conor also turned his gaze toward the mage, then to the Duke. "If wishing could make it so, My Lord, why then do you need me?" he asked, letting them both know he knew at least part of their secret.

The Duke sighed. "Would it were that easy. But Constance is a young girl just into her teens. As such, she is both foolish and romantic. I fear she believes that she is in love and may have gone off to follow some Romany prince who came here a fortnight ago. His father's caravan camped outside our grounds for a week. They were different and exotic, he was dashing and charming. Constance was quite taken with him. He left, and now she is gone. But to answer your question, yes, I do have the means to force her return, but I would not have my daughter a prisoner in her own home. Find her, Sir Conor, and if she is happy and safe, give her this." Rayford handed Conor a ring. "Ask for hers in return. Tell her that she is my light, my life, and my heir and always will be. And should she choose to return, she may come and go freely. Return with her ring and you will be well rewarded. Of course, should Constance return with you of her own free will, you will be even more greatly rewarded."

It had to be asked. "And should she not be happy and safe, my lord?"

Rayford's face darkened. "Then bring me the Rom's head in a sack and I will do right by you."

Had Ismael not been distracted by a courtier seeking advice, had Rayford not been dismayed by the thought that maybe his daughter was not happy and safe, had Conor measured his words before replying, perhaps a great tragedy would have been avoided. As it was, Conor bowed before the duke and said,

"As you wish, my lord."

Conor straightened, took his leave of the duke, and left in search of a Romany caravan, not knowing what harm he had done with five small words uttered automatically.

A large group of travelers is not hard to find, not for one of Conor's training. It cannot help but leave signs of its passing—grass trampled by horses, earth disturbed by campgrounds, covered fires, and buried wastes. If one were patient, he could find these things then follow the trail to one's quarry. With what he both knew and suspected, Conor did not bother doing this. Instead, he let fall his reins and allowed his horse to wander where it will, trusting that the power of Rayford's wish would guide his steed onto the right path.

Three days later, Conor found the first signs of the Romany caravan. In another week, he came upon the camp.

Well did Conor appreciate the dangers of an armed man riding into a camp of those who did not know him. So that night he settled himself just outside their grounds, close enough that he could be seen, far enough that he would not be considered an immediate threat. The next morning, when three men came out from the camp, Conor sat watching their approach and made no move toward his sword.

"Greetings, friends," he shouted out, "a fine day is it not?"

"It is for some," said the oldest and obvious leader of the three, "for others it may not be. Such is the way of the world."

Conor noticed that the trio spaced themselves out so that, if he were to attack one, the other two could make quick work of him. "That is true. Every day, no matter how nice, is someone's last."

"Let us hope," the older man said, "that for you that day will be far off."

"For you as well, my friends. And for your lord. I trust he is well."

"He is, though plagued with curiosity. He wonders why a lone knight has been shadowing him and his tribe for the past several days."

"Because the lone knight is not a fool. He knows that he might be a match for one of your people, or maybe two, but not all of them. He wished to avoid any misunderstanding that might lead to … unpleasantness before he could deliver his message."

The older man nodded. "You are indeed no fool, my friend, but what message have you?"

"It is for your lord and it is from Duke Rayford, whose hospitality you have but recently enjoyed."

One of the younger two said something in a language not known to Conor and all three laughed. "He said," explained the leader, "what took you so long?"

Conor was soon enjoying breakfast with Danylo of the Rom, outside the leader's brightly painted wagon.

"She followed us, of course," Danylo explained. "Well do we know what would happen should one of our number abduct a noble's daughter. Any man's daughter for that matter. In truth, that can be worse. Your gentry would merely hang us or put us to the sword. Town and farm folk are much more … imaginative … in their concept of justice. But as I said, the lady Constance followed us, arriving one night declaring her love for one of my sons."

"When you were at the castle, did this son, shall we say, declare his love for Constance?"

Danylo shrugged. "They are both young, neither is unattractive. Who can say? But whatever happened there, here the young lady has been treated as an honored guest. She has the run of the camp, but is all the time properly chaperoned."

"Is she happy here? Does she want to stay?"

The Rom chief smiled. "She thinks so. I see the way she looks at my son. Already she sees him as her mate. But wait a week, friend Conor. Your lady is used to soft beds and fine foods. There are no soft beds in my camp, and while the food is good, it is but simple fare. Soon she will tire of us and wish to return. When that day comes, she will be escorted back, properly chaperoned, and not by any of my sons."

"And should the day not come, friend Danylo, what then?"

"New blood is always welcome, and my son will have a wife. Is that a problem?"

"Not at all. Duke Rayford wished only that his daughter be safe and happy. May I deliver his message to her?"

"Of course, then you are welcome as long as you wish to stay. Tonight, as we eat, you can tell us tales that we have never heard, and we will share our stories with you. Tomorrow or the next, you can return and reassure your duke that his daughter is safe with the Rom."

When Conor returned to the duchy, it was not as he'd left it. The Inn of the Full Moon and the village that it served were nothing but charred rubble and of the people who had resided there, none were left alive.

Hurrying to the duke's stronghold, the knight found the castle still standing, with no one on the battlements and the gates, as before, open. Inside the walls, however, were signs of battle and slaughter. Bodies were everywhere, most wearing the colors of Duke Rayford, a few in the leathers and armor of raiders from the north. No women, dead or alive, could be found.

Conor's first thought was of Constance as he said a prayer of thanksgiving that the girl's romantic fantasies had kept her safe. The next was of the Duke. He had yet to see Rayford's body and the knight wondered if he was lying dead somewhere or had been taken captive. His final thought was of the dark-skinned Ismael and the folly and cost of relying on magic. Like the duke's, the magician's body was nowhere in sight.

Conor addressed the open air. "Did your magic fail, Sir Mage, or did you tire of playing the servant and betray your master?"

The air shimmered before him. Dust motes rose from the ground and took human form. Conor drew his sword and waited. It was not long before the shape of Ismael stood before him.

"I am capable of many things, Sir Conor, but betrayal is not in my nature."

A wary Conor kept his sword point close to the young man. "Where is your duke, mage?"

"He was among the first to fall, cut down in the outer ward then dropped in the moat."

"What happened?"

"The raiders came from the north, some days after you left. They were on us so quickly, there was no time for my master to find me and make the wish that would have repelled them. His men were fighting and dying and, possibly with the hope that I would find him in time, he joined them in defense of the castle. By the time I could get to him, he was my master no longer."

"And what of the magic that has protected this land for two decades. What happened to that?"

"You took it with you, Sir Knight, and like a fool I let you."

Even amidst tragedy and death, a man must see to his own needs. Conor was at the end of a long journey and needed food and drink. Ismael led the knight to the kitchen where he made good use of what little the raiders had left behind.

"What do you mean," Conor asked as he ate, "that I took the magic with me? You had best explain yourself, Magician."

"Yes, I should do exactly that, explain *myself.*

"I told you before," Ismael said, "that I was not a magician. Rather, I am magic given shape and form. As you are of the earth, so we Djinn are of fire. Once we walked with men and spoke with angels. But we grew too proud and when we sinned we did not repent. For our sins, we were made the servants of man, our powers and being bound in vessels through which we may be commanded. My prison is a ruby set in a pendant. Whoever owns that owns me."

"How is it that you are still free of your prison, given that Rayford is no more?"

"He set me free of it. That is, I need not reside there until called upon but may walk free. When a new master claims me, I will return to the jewel."

"You said I took the magic with me when I left to find Constance. How could I, if Rayford commanded your magic?"

"As you guessed early on, I am commanded through wishes. Three at any one time to any one master. After obtaining my vessel from a fool boy who did not know what he possessed, Rayford's first wish was safe passage to this land."

"And his second was to be made duke?"

"No, Sir Knight, that he accomplished on his own. His second was that his duchy be forever safe from invaders and raiders. His third wish was for an heir. Since he asked only for an heir and was not specific, his daughter Constance was born."

"Three wishes then, Ismael. Your obligation to him was at an end. Why then were you still in his service?'

"I said, three wishes at any one time. His first wish, that of safe passage, was no longer needed. He was free to supplant that with another. He used this wish as needed."

"Such as wishing for someone to find his errant daughter. But that was his last wish, why then ..."

"His next to last wish, Conor. Do you recall your last words to him? I am ashamed to say that I did not until I felt the duke die."

Conor thought back. "He had given me my instructions. I was about to take my leave and said ... but ..."

"You said, to the duke, 'As you wish.' And by saying it in my presence, even though neither he nor I noted it, it became his wish, supplanting another."

"And that was to protect his duchy."

The djinn nodded. "The magic failed, the raiders came, and here we are."

"What of the pendant and your ruby. Where are they?"

"Taken as spoils, spoils that have yet to be divided. When they are, I will have a new master. One who will not be as kind and benevolent as was Rayford. May the God against whom I sinned help this land and its people."

On hearing the djinn's words, Conor stood. "We've little time, then."

"To do what?"

"What else? Find the raiders, retrieve the pendant, and avenge the duke. My careless words are partly to blame for his death and I mean to put things right."

After a day's preparation, Conor and Ismael set out. An unprotected land gave raiders little incentive to leave, so their trail was quickly found. Two nights later, so was their camp.

"How many men attacked the castle?" Conor asked as the two watched from a distance. Campfires were being lit and meals prepared.

"Three score, maybe a few more or less. Why?"

"I count only half that number, all men, none of the women from the castle. They must have split up. You are sure that your pendant is with this band?"

"It is not my pendant, but my prison, but yes. This close, I feel it calling to me."

Fires burned low and the men prepared for sleep.

"Have you any magic of your own, Ismael, or can it only be used in service to a master?"

"I cannot help you, if that is what you ask. And if by chance one of them should grab the pendant and call for help, I may be your death."

"There is little chance of that. Wait here and guard the horses."

"Where are you going?"

But there was no one to answer. Conor had slipped away.

The sentries standing watch were the first to die, a sharp knife across their throats silently stealing their lives away. Then Conor was among them, a trained fighter loose among tired, surprised men. Some had swords or clubs close to hand. These he cut down as they rose. A true knight, he would not slay unarmed men. He allowed the others to gather weapons. It mattered not. This time not they were not facing soldiers who had not seen real combat in over a decade. Conor was a warrior born and their number meant only that there were more of them to kill.

Conor fought mercilessly, dispassionately; holding off the berserker rage that his people could call up, knowing that he needed a few of them alive. He took some cuts and blows but they slowed him not, indeed, in the heat of battle he barely felt them.

Soon it was over, the cowardly having fled; the dead, dying, or injured lying at his feet. He bound what injuries he could, to the ones who would not survive their wounds Conor granted the mercy of his knife. From those who were still alive, he learned the fate of the women.

Ismael arrived shortly after the slaughter had ceased.

"You're alive," he said with some surprise.

"Of course. I am a knight of Scotia, raised and trained in the tradition of the Fiana and the Red Branch. I have fought and defeated greater odds than this rabble. That is why I did not wish your help."

"I had none to give," the djinn replied and began searching the bags of the fallen raiders.

"Don't bother," Conor said, "What you seek is not there, or if it is, it is not what you claim it to be. At any rate, it was at best merely a distraction, one not meant to be found so as to leave you free."

"You speak riddles, friend Conor."

"Do not call me friend, Ismael." The knight reached into a pocket of his tunic and brought out a small object. It was a brass whistle. The djinn's eyes widened. "Rather, call me master." Conor blew the whistle.

Ismael, who had been about to spring on Conor, stood straight and unmoving.

"Well?" Conor said, his voice sharp with command.

There was hatred in Ismael's voice as he replied, "Yes … Master." There was something else, a questioning, a wondering in his eyes. "You may ask your question."

"How, how did I not sense the vessel?"

"Because I did not wish it. Once I found it and knew it for what it was, I wished you to forget I had it and not sense it. That was my first wish, a wish I now rescind."

Memory came back to Ismael as Conor went on.

"I began to suspect that something was amiss when we spoke on my return. How was it that while the duke reached the raiders in time to be killed, you did not reach him in time to save him? And after you explained to me your nature, I wondered, was it likely that Rayford would leave his most prized possession out where anyone could steal it? I thought not. He would have hidden it so that even the best thief could not find it. Unless Rayford was a fool or had grown careless.

"Either was possible. Then I remembered how you suddenly appeared to me when I returned to the castle. Could it be that your vessel was still close at hand? Maybe it was something that did not appear to be worth stealing, like a child's toy left carelessly on a table at his bedside.

"And how was it that a djinn, who must hear the wish to grant it, was not aware of the one that cost Rayford his life and dukedom? You heard it and chose not to warn your duke. Were you waiting for such a slip? Did you then send word to the raiders that the way was now clear?"

"And why would I do all this?"

"Because," Conor answered, "you hate us. You hate us for your servitude, you blame us for your slavery. In that, I cannot blame you. But neither can I forgive your actions. Rayford was a good man who treated you as well as he could, and you betrayed him."

One look at the djinn and Conor knew that he was right. Hatred for all humanity was in his eyes. The knight knew he must choose his words carefully lest any be used against him.

"I wish you to speak the truth. Are you my servant until someone else claims the vessel?"

"You are ... Master."

"Then as a true knight and one who served the duke of this land, I claim the right to mete out justice in his name. Hear then these wishes, Ismael the Djinn.

"I wish that the women who were abducted from the castle be returned to this land with no further harm coming to them.

"I wish that those who would have sold them into bondage and slavery suffer the fate they had planned for the women.

"I wish that this duchy once again be forever safe from invaders and raiders.

"As I have spoken, let it be done."

And along with the hatred in Ismael's eyes, Conor saw something else, a small glimmer of hope as the djinn allowed himself a brief smirk. The knight knew what he was thinking.

Those were your three wishes. One more will cancel the last, and the land will again run red with blood.

Conor allowed him that small victory as he blew the whistle to return the djinn to his vessel.

Loading the looted treasure on the raiders' horses, Conor returned to the castle where he found that some of the duchy's survivors had begun the gruesome task of burying the dead. The duke's body had been retrieved and placed in a crypt to await formal burial. Taking charge, Conor sent a party in the direction of the Romany caravan, to find Constance and break the sad news that she was now a duchess.

Acting as regent until Constance's return, Conor soon received word that the women taken from the castle had escaped and were on their way home. The same report told him that those who would have sold them had themselves been captured and taken into bondage.

Constance soon returned and with her, all of Danylo's tribe. She brought with her good news to lighten the bad, for love had bloomed during her stay with the caravan and soon the land would have a Romany duke.

But before there could be a wedding there first must be a funeral. The remains of Duke Rayford were respectfully removed and placed in the finest coffin the Rom craftsmen could construct. One by one, all present gave him final honors. As he was about to be lowered into the ground, no one noticed Conor slipping a small brass whistle into the coffin as he closed its lid. Later, after all had left, he stood alone at the duke's gravesite.

"Can you hear me, faithless one? If so, know that there will be no more wishes, no new masters. My judgment on you is an eternity of darkness alone with the one you betrayed." Soon after, Conor left the Duchy of the Rom. He had a finer horse than the one on which he had arrived, a gift from the new duke. His purse was filled with gold, a thank you from the new duchess. The road was clear and the days ahead promised adventure. It was, he thought, all that man could wish.

LOCAL CATCH

He sang of joy—joy of life, joy of the sea, the joy he would find at the end of his journey. There he would meet his mate and he would know her by the way she sang. Bonded forever, they would raise young and teach them the old songs and help them create their own.

His had been a long trip, one that was nearly over. Looking toward its end, he failed to sense the danger around him. Ensnared, he was lifted into the harsh light of the Above. Blinded at first, his eyes quickly adapted to the brightness around him.

Then came something sharp and shiny. Darkness fell around him for the last time. His song ended.

The water was cold against her skin. She had heard the song and had no choice but to respond to it. It spoke of romance and of finding one's true love. It promised pleasure beyond that which she had already known. It offered a chance to be reborn, a baptism into a new life.

Shedding what little she was wearing, she swam toward the song. Entranced by its melody, she failed to sense the danger around her. Taken suddenly, she was dragged Below. Sharp edges began their work.

The water turned red as darkness fell around her, the song changing to one of grim satisfaction. Then she heard it no more.

It was in a time before a knight known as Conor of Scotia became a hero, a time when he was just a wandering man-at-arms looking for adventure. He had just come from the Middle Kingdoms where he learned to be careful for what he wished—and how he wished. Riding west then south, the knight soon came to the shores of the Great Sea.

Sainte-Paul was just another town on the edge of that sea. Conor had no special reason for stopping save that both he and his horse were tired. Tired of his journey, tired of his own cooking, tired of sleeping on hard ground with only his steed for company. He wanted hot food, a hotter bath, a soft bed, and maybe even softer companionship. He hoped to find all four in the first tavern he saw.

Sainte-Paul was typical of the towns he had found in the south of Francia. An easy approach—no guards, no walls, nothing to keep anyone out. Much different from his native land, where every stranger was a possible enemy until proven otherwise.

Still, the town's trusting appearance was belied by the stares of its people. Some viewed him with curiosity. This Conor understood, guessing that it was not often that a man-at-arms rode through their streets on a battle charger. Others, though, glared at him with suspicion or even hatred and still others turned from him in fear.

For a moment Conor thought to remain on his horse and continue on to the next town. He might have, if he could have been sure of reaching it before dark. His reluctance to spend another night outdoors and the sudden appearance of an inn decided him. He would stay the night in Sainte-Paul.

Leaving his horse tied outside, Conor entered the inn. Ignoring the sudden silence that his appearance caused, he walked to the bar.

"Ale, please," he said in the language of Francia, one of the many he had had to learn as part of his training, "and a room with a bath, if you please. And have someone see to my horse."

The innkeeper hesitated but his reluctance faded when one of the knight's silver pieces landed on the bar's surface. All that was left was his surprise; surprise that someone from the barbaric North could not only speak a civilized tongue but wanted to bathe.

"Yes, good knight, we have a room, one that was cleaned only two days ago and has not yet been slept in. And we can most certainly prepare you a bath before you retire. But as for ale, good sir, alas, we have only wine."

Conor smiled, for a minute he had forgotten where he was. "The wine of this country is worth the journey, landlord. A cup to start with if you please and food to go with it. Keep both coming until the bathwater is good and hot."

The wine Conor was served was excellent and his meal of fish and fresh greens even better.

"Landlord," the knight asked as his cup was being filled for the third time, "this fish is, without any doubt, the best I have ever tasted."

"Thank you, sir, it is a … local catch."

Conor would have inquired further but just then four armed

men came through the door. Dressed uniformly, they seemed to be part of the town's Watch.

Trouble, Conor thought as three of the men walked toward him, the fourth remaining close to the door.

Loosening his sword in its scabbard, Conor thought again, *Trouble*. On studying them as they approached, he added, but nothing that can't be handled. He hoped that the landlord had not had time to take his horse to the stable.

"You will come with us," demanded the man in the middle.

Deliberately ignoring them, Conor took a last drink of wine and what would probably be his last bite of the excellent fish. Finally, he looked up and said,

"No."

"That was not a request. You will come with us."

Without bothering to rise Conor said, "Gentlemen, I know all too well the probable fate of a stranger, a foreign stranger, when he surrenders himself to the Watch. I do not wish to suffer that fate."

With one swift move, Conor overturned the table at which he was sitting, drawing his sword as he rose. A knife appeared in his left hand.

"I am Conor of Tuam, a knight of Scotia, son of Seamus, son of Liam, son of Conor. I am of the Fianna and trained with the Red Branch. Gentlemen, while I do not know how many men it would take to bring me down, the four of you are not enough. If, however, you think otherwise, I'll give you time to draw your weapons. The survivor can reimburse the landlord for the damages."

The man in charge had not made sergeant by taking chances or being stupid. Surmising that all the men of the Watch together might not be enough to defeat the man whose blade was dangerously close to his stomach he quickly came to a decision.

"Perhaps I misphrased my request, good knight. I had meant merely to ask your assistance in a matter most urgent. A man of your obvious training and experience would be invaluable in an investigation of ours."

Conor lowered but did not sheath his sword. "As your beautiful language is not my native tongue, perhaps it is I who misunderstood you, sir. Let it not be said that a knight of Scotia did not respond to a request for help. But …"

"Yes?"

"But first, let's have some wine and more of that excellent fish. And then I think, a bath."

Conor was glad that he had eaten before seeing the body, or rather, half a body. It was the upper torso of a young woman.

"Where's the rest of her, Sergeant Philippe?"

Philippe shrugged. "Who can say? We found this much of her on the beach this very morning. As you were the only armed stranger in town you can see why we …"

The knight nodded. "Understandable. I may have made the same mistake. Who is she?"

Another shrug. "She has been in the water for some time. With the damage to her face, we may never know."

There are other ways of identifying a body, Conor thought as he looked at this one. Already he had seen one or two marks that someone … intimate with the poor woman might recognize.

"Anyone missing from your town, Sergeant?"

"My men have already checked, Conor. No one. And I have sent word to the neighboring towns asking that same question."

"Very good. Now before heat and time begin their work on this poor unfortunate, may I suggest bringing in the single men of this village, and possibly those married ones who may at times forget their vows, to see if they might have known this woman."

"But how? As I have said, her face, it is … oh." Philippe shook his head. "It would not be right, to expose her like that."

"She is past caring, Philippe, and it was not right for her to die as she did."

"Of course, I will make the arrangements."

After the sergeant left, Conor began a closer examination of the body. Excluding what ravages the sea had wrought, she bore no wounds on either her front or back. Perhaps she was drowned then butchered, he hoped so, but the knight knew of only one way to be sure of that and he needed what was left of her torso intact.

What tool was used, the knight wondered. Familiar with most types of edged weapons, Conor knew that no straight blade had been used. Judging from the damage, whatever had done the job was sharp but jagged. He thought maybe a chirurgeon's saw, but even that left smoother marks than what he found on the backbone.

"Conor," came Sergeant Philippe's voice from the doorway, "I have brought some men and more are on their way."

"Good. Anyone refuse?"

"Not a one. Most are anxious to view the remains, they are … curious." This last was said with just a trace of disgust.

"They are human, Philippe." Draping a sheet over the area where the woman's lower body should have been he added, "Send them in."

"There's one thing, the priest is here. He wishes to be present."

"Tell the good father to pray for her soul, we'll tend her body. Now send in the men one at a time."

An hour went by, then two. Some of the men lingered, as to memorize this once-in-a-lifetime sight. Others hurried past, barely glancing at the body. None showed any sign of recognition or guilt. Conor thought back to the Druids of his homeland who believed that in the presence of the killer a murdered body would arise and point. As much as he had argued with them, Conor wished one of those Druids were with him now.

Another dozen or so men had walked past when a youth entered the room. He was of that age that is between boy and man and just as the others like him had done, he walked past slowly and reverently, as if a great mystery was being revealed. Unlike the others, he reached out and gently touched the woman's arm.

"Philippe," the knight called out, "hold the line." Then to the youth, "What is your name, boy?"

"Etienne, Sir."

"You know her, don't you? You *knew* her, didn't you?"

Understanding the implication, the boy nodded. "Her name is, was Anne. She is from Sainte-Pierre, the next town over. We met one day. I had never … she was my first … I was her … her latest. She showed me what it was like to be a man and now she's …"

Seeing that the youth was close to tears, Conor pulled the sheet completely over the body. "I have to ask, Etienne, how do you know that it is she?"

"She has … two moles … here." He indicated her left breast.

Conor nodded. He had seen them, known that a lover could not have failed to note them.

"Thank you. You may go, but speak nothing of this to anyone."

When the boy had gone, Conor called in the sergeant. "Philippe, come in, if you please."

When the officer appeared, the knight said, "Her name is Anne, the boy Etienne, well, you know how soon boys think they become men."

Philippe nodded. "One of my men has just returned from Sainte-Pierre. A woman by that name has not been seen for some days. It seems she was a very giving woman, one who shared her favors easily." He looked at the body. "Jealousy?"

"If so, jealousy mixed with madness, a dangerous combination."

"What is also dangerous, friend Conor, is a woman from one town found in ours. And a young man who knew her intimately if but briefly. There could be trouble."

"That kind of trouble can be handled. Now if you would, please bring in the priest to administer the last sacrament. If he objects, remind him of the Magdalene."

That evening, the boy Etienne stood on the shore where the woman's upper body was found and looked over the water. He had sinned, or so he believed. It had not seemed like a sin at the time, but now … he remembered the words of the priest from the pulpit, words about the sins of the flesh. He had not understood at the time but now he did. They had sinned, he had sinned, and Anne had paid the price.

"She was the bigger sinner," said a small voice inside him. "She had been with many men, she led you into sin. It was not your fault, not your sin."

As young as he was, Etienne knew this to be a lie. Anne, poor sweet Anne, had not led him anywhere. He had gone willingly. It was their sin, not just hers but she alone had paid.

Then he heard it, a song that played to his heart. It sang of love found and lost, of joy and sorrow, of pain and redemption. Looking around, the boy could not find its source, then realized from where it came.

The song called to him and he had no choice but to answer.

Without pausing to remove his clothes, Etienne walked into the sea to wash the stain from his soul.

At his table in the tavern, Conor tried to think of what to do next. Sergeant Philippe's men had begun questioning the citizens of Sainte-Paul, hoping to find someone who had seen the woman Anne and, more importantly, anyone who may have been with her. Even knowing what trouble it might cause, he had also asked the Watch of Sainte-Pierre to inquire of its citizens about the movements of the victim and any strangers, outsiders, or jealous lovers.

Not for the first time did the knight wonder what he was doing, why he had remained to help in this matter. He was just a man with a sword, not a hero or wizard of whom the bards sang. One of them would have spotted the killer right away and after a chase and maybe a beautiful maiden or two in peril, there would have been a great duel during which the villain would be vanquished and after which one of the maidens would have been most grateful.

But this was not one of those tales. There were no heroes, the victim, may her soul rest easy, was certainly no maiden and the villain was likely to be caught purely by chance. No, this was not one of those tales.

Thinking of tales caused Conor to remember something from earlier that morning. He was tending his horse when he saw the landlord with an enormous fishtail. He had wondered at the time if that was the "local catch" that the man turned into such a delicious meal. He had also wondered what had happened to the other half of the fish.

Half a fish and half a woman. Sitting at the tavern table Conor could not help put the two together. If the victim had not been identified he might have thought … but no. The knight had seen many strange things in his life but women from the sea were still the stuff of legends and stories told to children.

Even as Conor put such fanciful thoughts out of his mind he heard a watchman call his name.

"Conor, come at once. There's another one."

Led to the beach Conor saw two watchmen standing by a small figure. As the man who came to get him started toward the water, the knight held him back.

"Wait," he said. "Have you been down there?'

"No, sir."

"Then let's not disturb things any more than they need be. Wait here and keep the curious from coming down."

Taking a roundabout way to the body, Conor studied the sand, seeing only two sets of footprints. Nor had he seen anymore by the time he reached the water's edge.

Sergeant Philippe and one other stood over the body. Looking down, Conor saw that it was Etienne's. He had been killed in the same manner as had Anne. Choking down what he was feeling—horror, uselessness, a sense that he had somehow failed the boy, the knight asked,

"Has anyone been down here?"

Both men shook their heads.

"Yours, and now mine, are the only tracks." Looking out over the water, Conor added, "Whoever it was came from the sea."

An idle thought of the merpeople crossed his mind. The knight chased it away with,

"Who knew about the boy?"

"Only us," Philippe said.

"Anyone from Sainte-Pierre might have seen them together." The watchman said in anger. He ran off after he said this.

"I'll stay with the body, Philippe. You try to stop that hothead before it's …."

The news had spread. A crowd had gathered. Even now the watchman who had been with Conor and Philippe was talking to them, exhorting them, riling them up.

"… too late."

Some of the crowd remained. Others followed the watchman.

"They will be going toward Sainte-Pierre, to seek revenge for Etienne." The sergeant looked down at the body. "Just as I am sure that there are those in that town who blame us for the death of one of their own. There will be blood spilled today."

"Enough blood has been spilled, Philippe. Remain here. I'll send someone to help you with the boy."

Riding ahead of the angry townspeople, Conor intercepted it just moments before they met a similar mob from Sainte-Pierre. The sight of the armed knight gave both groups pause.

Now, this is something I can handle, Conor thought, *at least I hope I can.*

As he had told Sergeant Philippe, Conor did not how many men it might take to bring him down. But from the size of both mobs there looked to be enough. Still, they were just townsfolk and he a trained knight. And part of his training was how to avoid a messy fight.

"Who wants to die today?" Conor shouted loud enough for all to hear. When there were no replies except whispers and mumbling, he shouted again,

"Who wants to die today? Let him step forward and I will grant his wish."

Again there were no replies. No one stepped forward.

"Then return to your homes. Let the Watch handle this."

"But they killed Etienne," called the watchman who had incited the Sainte-Paul mob. Some of the people behind him murmured their agreement.

"Who did?" the knight asked. "Point them out and I will slay them for you."

The watchman grew silent. Conor turned to the crowd from Sainte-Pierre.

"And is there anyone you want killed for the death of the woman Anne?"

There is one in every crowd. This one shouted back, "Someone has to pay."

"Someone will," the knight replied. "But not now, not today. Go home. Two deaths are enough. Do not seek to add more to this tragedy."

Their anger defused for now, the two mobs slowly dispersed. Conor waited for all to leave, the last to go being the watchman who had started it all. Giving the knight a sullen look, he too finally departed.

"That one will bear watching," Conor said to his horse. "But that is Philippe's problem. Mine is to make good on my pledge that two deaths are enough."

The torsos of both bodies had been found on the beach. Despite an exhaustive search of the homes and countrysides of both towns, the remaining parts of neither victim were located. Nor had any fresh graves been found. It seemed to Conor that, for whatever reason, the killer had consigned the lower halves of the victims to the sea.

With that thought in mind, Conor set up a vigil on the beach. The night was cold, and as full as the moon was, it shed light but no heat. With only a blanket for warmth, the knight stood his lonely watch and looked out over the waters of the Great Sea.

A flash of silver. At first, Conor thought he might have imagined it but then saw it again. A flash in the moonlight. Staring out over the water he both saw and heard it, a great tail rising out of then slapping the surface of the sea.

"Local catch," he quietly said to himself, marveling at the size of the fish.

Then he heard the music. It came from over the waves and wafted onto the shore. It sang to Conor of love and passion, promising to fulfill his most ardent desires. The song shifted and became one of the glories that could be achieved if only one sought them out. A third tune told of the treasures of the deep, waiting for one brave man to dive deep and claim them.

He was tempted, Conor was. A young man still, he had never found true love, and the song of passion fulfilled drew him toward the water's edge.

As a boy in Tuam he had heard tales of brave heroes and great kings, and so was inspired to become a knight. And what knight does not want to hear his own praises sung? Thoughts of glory drew him closer to the water.

And what man could not use treasure? If not for now, then to set aside for his later years when his body can go no more a roaming.

Without realizing it, Conor found himself at the water's edge. But for recent events, he might have continued until he was under the sea, his armor dragging him to the bottom. But he had learned in the Middle Kingdoms that nothing comes without a price and that promises were no more solid than the air on which they came.

His training saved him. Knights of the Red Branch are taught how to defend themselves against many kinds of danger, those that threaten the soul as well as the body. They are also taught arts other than those of battle and war.

"Close." Looking around, Conor saw a rocky outcropping jutting into the water. Carefully walking out on it, he let his voice drift over the sea. "Now let me sing you one."

Suspecting now that the legends were true, that the sirens of the sea were more than just a children's tale, Conor sang his own song.

His voice was not pretty. It would never successfully woo a fair maid unless she had already decided to be won. His was a warrior's voice, heard best in the mead hall after a hard-won battle and far too much ale. Still, he sang.

Conor sang of a woman whose joy in life was sharing that joy with others. He sang of a boy whose first step toward manhood had been his last. He sang of sadness—the sadness of loved ones, the ache that each death leaves in the hearts of those who remained.

His song echoed and left an ache in his own heart. Never had he felt the pain and sorrow of death and loss as he had that night. He learned of lovers ripped from one another, and how cruel fate returned the bodies of those lost to the sea.

The song from the sea shifted and became one of justice sought and vengeance found. And on that song, Conor suddenly knew all, knew that the legends were true, knew that more would be lured into the depths and why, knew what the local catch had been.

Even as his stomach churned with the thought of meals recently eaten, even acknowledging the rightness of the cause, he could not, would not allow any more innocents to die.

Conor sang of the deaths of those innocents and his intention to prevent more. His song was of a great fleet of fishing vessels sailing along the coast. He sang of nets and hooks and spears, of poisoned waters and Greek Fire. He sang of the black powder from Cathay that caused great destruction and how it could be made to work underwater. Conor sang of the cruelty of Man and how it would be employed against the peoples of the sea.

Unless … His voice hoarse, his stomach threatening to disgorge all of what he had eaten in the past few days, Conor sang of peace. He sang of deaths on both sides and justice that he himself would mete out.

Silence.

Had his song been heard? Had it been heeded? Or must he give the warning that would mean war between the land and the sea?

In the moonlight he saw them, heads and bodies of men and women. No, not quite. The eyes were not right. In the light of the moon, they shone somewhat like a cat's. And they did not have hair but tendrils. Their hands when raised were webbed. These were the Mer, no longer legend.

Two swam closer. Soon they too were up on the rocks, supported by their strong upper limbs. Conor could easily tell that one was male and the other female.

"Too many have died," came a voice like a song that was more in his head than his ears. Only by seeing her lips move could Conor tell that it was the mermaid who had spoke. He was about to agree when the merman added,

"Too many of the People. Your kind has separated lover from lover, mother from child, brother from sister. Blood has been spilled. More blood must follow."

"Your blood will follow. Your sea will fill with it. You have heard my song. It was no idle boast. Mankind is a cruel race when we are threatened. When we war on what we fear it is not to the death but to extinction."

"We have no choice, we know no other way." The two were about to slip away when Conor shouted,

"Hold."

When they did he asked, "Yours is a warrior race?"

"It is," came the musical voice of the sea maiden.

"I too am a warrior. I offer a warrior's challenge. Let us fight, here, tonight, for the fate of all."

"And how may that be?" she asked. "You cannot enter our world and we," raising herself up, she flashed her long silver tail, "cannot stand in yours."

"We have spears," offered the merman. "Stand on these rocks, human. If you can survive our throws, we would count you as victor and stop our predation. If you cannot, you go Below and so does your knowledge of us."

"How many throws?"

"Ten of ours were lost," replied the maid, "so that many throws."

"You killed two of my people," countered Conor, "eight throws."

"Agreed." The male slipped back into the sea. The female mer, however, remained.

"You wear a strange shell, human. It must all be removed before the challenge can commence."

Conor nodded. "But just the armor, my lady of the sea. The rest stays on."

Her mouth formed a disappointed frown, one that seemed to Conor to be universal among females no matter what species. "Pity, I had hoped …" Then she smiled, "If you survive this challenge, I may perhaps offer you a more difficult one."

There was no mistaking the invitation, or maybe it was a ploy to distract him with other thoughts. Briefly wondering if and how such a challenge could be met, Conor gave a knightly bow and replied,

"Then my lady, you have given me another reason to win."

Another smile, another flash of her tail and she disappeared beneath the waves.

Divesting himself of all armor but his sword and buckler, Conor stood ready to meet the challenge. He wondered from where the first throw would come. Heads appeared above the surface. Diversions, he thought as he weighed his chances.

About even. The mer were used to throwing underwater. Hitting a target on land might be more difficult. Or so he hoped.

He did not see the first spear coming. It flew over his head. The second splashed into the sea in front of the rocks.

Two gone, thought the knight even as he knew they were getting the range. Putting himself deeper into a warrior state of mind, he scanned the sea.

There, a head and an arm. He stopped that spear on his buckler. Turning quickly, he deflected another with his sword.

The fifth spear grazed his leg, a sixth came dangerously close to his head.

He sensed rather than heard the mer behind him. The male had climbed onto the rocks and was preparing to throw. Conor had little time to do else but drop flat as the spear passed over him.

A scream then cries of anguish filled his head. Had the last spear come he could not have blocked it. When he rose Conor saw why he still lived.

A merman was on the rocks. He had come close in order to use a short thrust to end the knight should the other spears fail. When Conor dropped, the seventh throw found him instead.

Letting go of his sword, the knight rushed to him and drew him up on the rocks.

Conor would have saved the mer if he could. As it was, all he could do was hold him as songs of mourning and loss filled the night.

A male's voice entered his mind. "It is over. You are the victor."

"There is no victor here," Conor said as he handed the dead mer back to his own kind. "And it is not over."

When the sun rose the next morning there was no one at the inn save the landlord and Conor.

"You have arisen early, Sir Knight. Some of our local catch to break your fast?"

"I think not. I … have lost my taste for fish. Come, landlord, and sit beside me." Conor threw a silver piece on the table to tempt the man. When he was seated,

"I spoke with the Mer last night."

"The who, good sir?"

"The Mer, the People of the Sea. The source of your 'local catch.' Are you telling me you did not know?"

A lie almost came from the landlord's mouth. The look on the knight's face stopped it. A shake of his head established the landlord's guilt.

"Who else? Your wife?"

Again the landlord shook his head. Conor allowed him the lie.

"Who brings them to you?"

"There is this fisherman. By accident, he found their spawning ground. He is skillful with his net. He brings us what he catches."

"He supplies only you?"

The landlord shrugged. "Who can say?"

"Tell me his name and when I find him, he will."

It was then that both men became aware of noises coming from out front.

"That would be the folk of both towns gathering. I had Philippe spread the word that I might have word of the murderer today. Good sir, you have a choice. I can march you outside and give you to them, those people who just yesterday were ready to slaughter each other because of these deaths. Or we can slip out the back."

Conor allowed the landlord a moment of hope before adding, "So I can give you to the Mer. I understand that they have ways of keeping a man from drowning, of allowing him just enough air to live on while his body feeds their young. Your choice."

"What of my wife?"

Conor looked at the front door. "That way and she at least gets to live." Then to the back. "That way, I make no promises."

Together the two men walked out the front of the tavern. A quick hanging followed.

Conor paid one last visit to the rocks on the shore. In the moonlight, he sang of justice done and then of a fishing ship, a location, and a time. Together, he sang, they would end this.

Two days later, on a dock not too far from Sainte-Paul, Conor stood watching a fishing ship burn. Boarding the ship by force of arms, he had found the evidence of the crew's guilt—a dead mer about to be cut in two. That's when he fired the ship, but not before giving the ship's captain and his men a choice—they could face the flames or his sword, or take their chance in the water. He did not say what fate awaited those who chose the latter.

With hooks and gaffs, two decided to face his steel. They lay dying at his feet. Seeing their comrades fall, the other crewmen jumped overboard.

That's when the screaming started. It quickly stopped when the men were dragged under.

The captain was the last to die. Rejecting the flames, the sea, and the knight's sword, the captain drew his own blade and ended his life. As the flames consumed the corpse, Conor prayed that there were hotter fires awaiting him.

And so it is ended, Conor thought as he walked down to the sea. He listened for a moment, expecting a song.

At first, there was none. Then as he turned to leave, a lone voice sang to him, telling him of a place and a time and a challenge yet to be met.

A *Knight of the Red Branch*, Conor thought, *should not deny a lady, nor should he refuse a challenge.* Eager and curious, he sang back his acceptance.

The Good, the Bard, and the Ugly

Conor of Scotia walked through the fair of Nieves enjoying the dry air and warm weather. Elsewhere storms raged, storms that kept him from boarding a ship and crossing the Norman Sea to Carney, and from there to Caerleon where he hoped to meet brothers-in-arms and perhaps revive an ancient tradition. That the rain and wind had not visited itself on the town and fairgrounds might have been explained by luck. However, the "after storm" smell and a certain tingling in the air told the knight that it was more likely magic at work, magic that guaranteed good weather for the fair at the expense of foul weather elsewhere.

He confirmed this when he sought a room at the Stone Moon Inn. "It's the Wizard's doing," the landlord explained. "Two seasons ago the rains came and washed us all out. No money was to be made that year. And this town depends on what the fair brings in. So does the Wizard, for he gets a share of our earnings. Since then, well, look outside. Even those who don't care to make merry come to Nieves if only to escape the foul mess outside it."

"And the fact that others pay the price for your good weather?"

"What do you think? Look around, my inn is full and I'll make enough to carry me until spring. Yes, I know there's no such thing as a free meal, but as long as I don't have to pay the piper's tune it's all right with me. And even if it wasn't..." the landlord looked in the direction of the Wizard's keep, "...it's all right with *him* and there's naught anyone can do about that."

Conor knew differently. As a wandering knight and sometimes sword-for-hire, he had fought and overcome magic and its users. But he said nothing. It was not his fight. He had stopped at Nieves only because he had to.

"But enough talk about the weather," the landlord said. "What else can I get you? Another ale?"

Conor nodded. "That and a room. From what you tell me I'm here until the fair is over and the weather breaks."

The ale was good and easily poured. The room was somewhat harder to come by. Crowded as the inn was, as all the inns were, Conor settled for a space on the floor of the common room. It was better than sleeping outside, not that it was likely to rain, at least until the week was done.

So with nothing to do and a week to do it in, Conor walked the fair, enjoying what entertainment there was and examining the goods for sale. Most of the latter were from the locals but there were vendors from other parts of the continent as well. A couple from Stratford with what they claimed were pixies in a cage. A brewer from Corning. Conor was at the stall of a leathersmith's trying to decide whether to replace his worn scabbard when he heard:

"Don't walk by. Come, hear the stories. Welcome all to the big, fat, wonderful world of me!"

Conor turned toward the noise. On a makeshift stage, he saw a large man in modified jester's garb enticing people to gather round with promises of songs and stories—told and sung for a price of course.

"He's been at that all day," the smith complained. "Every half hour the same rant. It's getting so if he should suddenly go mute, may the saints will it so, I could step in and say it for him."

"But is he any good? Are his tales worth the telling?"

"Who can say? Once the crowd is large enough and there's money in his bowl, his voice drops so that only those who paid can hear him. Now about that hide you hold in your hand. I can fashion you a nice scabbard from that in no time at..."

But the knight was not listening, his attention now on the storyteller. "Thank you," he told the smith absently. "I'll think about it and be back."

"I've heard that before."

A small group had gathered around the stage, mostly children whose parents had left them while they shopped or sold. The bowl in front of the storyteller was mostly empty, the few coins in it either brass or debased copper.

The minstrel sighed. "For this, I could tell a short tale of pirates or dragons."

"Pirates *and* dragons," suggested a young lad in the crowd.

"Would that I could, young sir, but the length of the story depends on the coins in the bowl, and for what I see before me I could only…" he looked out, appealing to what few adults were standing behind the children. No help was forthcoming. Unable to disappoint an audience, no matter its size or age, the storyteller sighed and said, "Perhaps I could tell the tale of Jac and Her Beanstalk."

There were moans and groans and cries of "Not again" and "We've heard that one." And indeed they had, for it had been told twice before and mostly to the same crowd of children.

Conor could wait no longer. "Hold up, Sir Bard," he called and walked up to the stage. Drawing a gold coin from his purse, he dropped it in the bowl. "Your finest tale if you would, one of sword, sorcery, and daring deeds. A lengthy tale, one suitable for these fine young people."

Smiling in delight at the coin that shone in the bowl, the storyteller winked and said;

"Many thanks, Sir Knight. What is your name so I can sing your praises at a later time and perhaps add you to a tale or two?"

"I am Conor of Scotia and you do me honor by accepting my coin. In my country, bards and shanachies are revered and it is considered a duty and privilege to support them."

"We are well met, Sir Conor. I am called Seejay, son of Hender and if what you say is true then when this fair is over I may travel with you, if you will have me."

"Let us talk of that another time, Sir Bard. For now, you have young folk waiting for a great tale."

"About that, Sir Conor. While the tale I'm about to tell is complete in itself, it would be even better with song. For another coin…"

Laughing, Conor added silver to the gold then sat with the children to enjoy the tale of Princess Eliza and the Dragon Lord. The Bard even made sure to include a few pirates. And in no time at all Seejay had his audience laughing, crying, and singing along.

The noise of enjoyment from the small crowd drew a larger one, then one larger still. Within two turns of the glass, it seemed that half the fair had gathered around Seejay's stage where he talked, sang, told jokes, and danced like a monkey whenever a small coin was added to the now-overflowing bowl.

Enjoying himself more than he had since leaving his native land, Conor sat through tales of Jacques of The Hague and London Teddy before deciding to see the rest of the fair. Thanks to Seejay, there were fewer buyers around the other vendors and so Conor was able to bargain for better prices on food, drink, and some of the goods he would need for his journey. A man of his word, he did return to the pleasantly surprised leathersmith and commissioned a new scabbard to be delivered at fair's end.

Night came and the fair closed. While most vendors were closing their booths and covering their wares, Conor heard, "Sir Conor."

Turning, he saw the storyteller walking toward him. "Master Seejay, was it a good day for you?"

"One of the best, though it could always be better. Still, I am weighed down by the coin that came my way. Could I perhaps trouble you to escort me? I hear there are thieves about, and I speak not just of some of the vendors."

"Again, it is my honor. And as a bard stands higher than a simple knight, call me Conor."

"And I am to one and all simply Seejay."

"Where are you staying?"

The bard at least had the grace to look sheepish before saying, "The thing is, I failed to make arrangements for proper lodging. Perhaps I could share yours? I'll take up as little room as possible and I do not snore, at least, I have never heard myself doing so."

Again the knight laughed. "You can share whatever part of the floor the landlord has allotted me."

"The floor? Not even a couch?"

"The floor it is. Of course, your golden tongue can probably talk the landlord out of his bed and into leaving his wife behind."

Seejay smiled at the challenge. "I might at that. A bed would be nice, but as for the wife, tonight I am too tired."

As Conor had expected, the Inn of the Stone Moon was already crowded. Ale and wine flowed and the exhausted barmaids grew tired of serving drinks and dodging the drinkers.

Catching the landlord's eye, Conor told him of the great honor that had been bestowed upon his establishment. The famed storyteller, the most celebrated bard of the continent, the very talk of the Nieves's Fair, had deigned to visit his inn, and for the small price of a comfortable place to sleep and enough mead and ale to keep his throat wet, he would entertain his guests and keep them eating and drinking until the watch ordered the inn closed. When the landlord hesitated, Conor added, "Or Seejay Hender's son can go elsewhere, but I cannot guarantee that he will not draw your patrons away with him. As I am staying here, it would pain me to have to eat and drink alone."

The landlord quickly agreed to the knight's terms. On hearing what Conor had done, Seejay was, for once, speechless. Once he found his voice, his only words were, "How?"

"You are a bard, I took training with them. I can tell a tale when I must."

"And a pretty tale it was. Now let us eat and drink before," Seejay looked at the crowd, "I must get to work." He sighed as if being the center of attention was a great burden to him.

After he had eaten, Seejay began earning his keep by singing a few songs. His rendition of "Stab Them in the Back" soon had most of the crowd, especially what guardsmen were present, singing along. He then told a tale about two men who journeyed to the moon in a giant saucer, until finally he said, "More later. My throat is dry and demands ale. But while I satisfy my thirst, I present to you a young knight, one trained not only by the feared Red Branch itself but by the very bards of Scotia. He will tell you stories of his great deeds."

Unlike Seejay, Conor did not like to be noticed. He would have demurred but as a knight he was trained to meet all challenges. So while the storyteller ate and drank, Conor told of a genie who betrayed his master and was then bested by one more clever than he. He followed this with a tale of the merfolk and how a near war between land and sea was narrowly averted. While speaking, he noticed that Seejay listened intently, no doubt making mental notes of the knight's stories so he could add them to his repertoire. Conor ended with a bawdy song about a mermaid and a tortoise before nodding to Seejay that it was again his turn.

"Well," began the storyteller, "as my friend and companion has told a tale of the sea and sang a song about a *tail* of the sea," he waited while those who got the jest laughed, "allow me to continue the theme.

Has anyone here present heard of the Deep Ones?"

Conor had, as part of his knightly training. In his travels, he had heard them spoken of in whispers and rumors. Conor looked around. Everyone else shook their heads; all save two guardsmen who began listening intently. Seejay spoke of the fish-like creatures that lured men to destruction with promises of gold and power.

The bard's story ended with the navy of the Doge of Venice using Greek Fire to eliminate a town that had been overrun by the creatures. On seeing his audience's fascination with such horrors he began telling of the Old Gods, beings forgotten by creation, cast out of existence, and now lurking on the other side of the world's threshold, waiting to again enter and devour all.

Seejay was speaking of a Sleeper whose awakening would mean the end of all when one of the guardsmen nodded to another. The one who nodded then left but not before saying something to his fellow. Although Conor could not hear what was said by their actions he imagined it was something like "Watch him. I'll bring the others." The knight hoped he was wrong but loosened his sword in its scabbard just in case.

A turn of the glass and Seejay was still speaking. Conor was only partly listening, instead alternately watching the remaining guardsman and the inn door, waiting for something to happen. From what little the knight heard the bard's story was one of fairies and cockroaches.

"Enough for now," the storyteller announced, "for I need my rest if I am to thrill the fairgoers tomorrow with tales of daring deeds."

"One more," shouted several members of his audience.

"I don't know…"

A coin hit the floor near Seejay, then several others.

"Well, if you insist. In the opening days of the Trojan War, an ominous tome falls into the hands of the Trojan High Command. Can our heroes …."

"Seejay, son of Hender …" interrupted a voice from the doorway.

Damn, thought Conor as what was clearly a lieutenant of the guards stepped into the inn. Several guardsmen followed. The one who had remained behind moved to join them.

"Seejay, son of Hender," the lieutenant said again.

"Do you mind? I'm in the middle of a story. If there's a tale you wish told, then come to the fair tomorrow and drop a coin in my bowl."

"You will come with us," the lieutenant said as if the storyteller had not spoken.

Damn, the knight again thought, then stood. "Where are you taking him and by whose authority?" he demanded of the lieutenant.

"What business is it of yours?"

"This man, this noble bard, this honored storyteller, is under my protection."

By now the crowd that had gathered around Seejay to hear his tales dispersed as best they could. Some went upstairs, others hid under the tables, most hugged the walls.

"And who are you and why should I care?"

"I am Conor, a knight of Scotia, son of Seamus, son of Liam, son of Conor and you should care because I will not permit this man to be taken where he does not wish to go." Turning to Seejay, Conor asked,

"Do you wish to go with them?"

Seejay shook his head. "It has been my experience that going with guardsmen in the middle of the night seldom leads to pleasant consequences. I would just as soon stay with you."

"It matters not what either of you wish. The Wizard Maldon demands this man's presence in his Keep."

"Seejay?"

"I would still rather not."

"Behind me then."

"Sir," Conor said to the lieutenant. "Please tell your master that Bard Seejay will await his pleasure tomorrow on the fairgrounds. If it is a story he wants, the bard will tell it gratis, in thanks to the Wizard for hosting the fair in such pleasant weather. Anything else can be discussed at that time."

The lieutenant shook his head. "That, Sir Knight, is not an option."

Conor's hand went to his sword. "Then blood must be spilled."

With Seejay safely behind him in a corner, Conor positioned himself so that the guardsmen could come at him only singly or in pairs. He tried not to kill, recognizing that his foes of the evening were simply men doing their job. He wounded when he could but there were those who fell never to rise again. Slowly he reduced his enemy.

A dozen became nine, then six, then three until there was only one.

"Well fought, Sir Knight," the lieutenant of the guard said. "I told the Wizard that the Guard would be no match for one such as yourself."

"Why fight me then?'

"Because the Wizard ordered me too. Because he needed time."

Conor did not ask "time for what?" As soon as the lieutenant spoke he knew that he had been duped, that the men he fought, the ones he had injured or killed, had been sent merely as a distraction. Behind him came a rumble, then the sound of air rushing through a hole. Conor did not have to turn around to know that Seejay was gone.

Anger almost took the knight. He nearly struck out with his sword to remove the lieutenant's head from his shoulders. But his training held. Anger in battle only got one killed.

"You have until daybreak to leave Nieves," the lieutenant told him. "Accept your defeat gracefully, Sir Conor, and move on. You did your best, but there is now nothing you can do to save your friend."

"I will give *you* until daybreak," Conor calmly replied, "to deliver my message to this Wizard Maldon. He has until tomorrow eve to return the Bard Seejay—unharmed, unspelled, and with a purse twice as heavy as he had when taken."

"Or..."

"Ask your master if he knows exactly of what a Knight of the Red Branch is capable. Our training goes deep. If I must, I will raise armies of the dead. I will call on the spirits of Faerie. I will mortgage my soul to whatever demon I must to fulfill my vow to one under my protection. Tell your master this. Tell him to return the bard or prepare for war."

Looking into the knight's eyes the lieutenant read the truth in what had been said. "I will tell him." He then looked past Conor at his fallen men.

"They will be cared for. Now go."

After the lieutenant left, those remaining gathered around Conor. They all began to talk at once.

"Are you really going to do all those things? Can you?...Will you usurp the Wizard?...You will be killed...You should leave; the storyteller is no doubt already dead...what of the fair?...What of my inn? Who's paying the damages…What about these men?

With a shout and a wave of his arms, Conor silenced them all. "The less you all know the better. Someone fetch a healer for the wounded. Landlord," gold and silver hit a table, "that should be payment enough for what is needed." Looking over the dead, Conor selected one. Picking up the corpse, he slung it over his shoulder.

"What do you want him for?" asked one of the wounded guardsmen.

Conor looked at the man with cold eyes. "Sometimes an offering is needed. Thank your gods that I do not need a living one." Addressing those remaining he said, "Warn your loved ones. Tomorrow will be a dark day. I go now to summon my forces and prepare for battle. Let none follow or disturb me."

There were moans behind the Wizard Maldon as he asked his Lieutenant of the Guard, "Do you believe him? Can he do all that he said he could?"

The moans gave way to tortured laughter. "Of course, he can," said the bound and bloody Seejay. "He's Conor of Scotia, the finest of the Red Branch Knights."

A slight movement of the Maldon's hand caused the bard to groan in pain.

"Silence!" commanded the wizard.

"Very well, if you don't want to know what you're facing."

"You would buy your freedom by betraying your friend?"

More weak laughter came from the bound man. "As if you would set me free without learning the secrets you think I have. No, I want you to know all of which Conor is capable so that you can see what doom awaits you."

Maldon held up his hand, then interrupted the gesture. "Speak, or I will roast the flesh from your leg an inch at a time."

"The man you face has overcome the might of the Djinn. He has plumbed the depths of the sea, defeated the Mer, and stolen away their women. He is named for the Hound, who held off Maeve's army single-handed and slew five men after he was dead. He is of the race of McCool and Patricus, who drove demons from the land. He was trained by warriors, priests, and druids. He is one of the most dangerous men on the continent and you have angered him. Release me or suffer. Kill me and you will beg for damnation."

Maldon turned to his lieutenant. "What say you? You took the measure of the man last night."

The lieutenant shrugged. "I know not, my lord. Perhaps. Why else would he take a corpse as an offering?"

"Find him. Stop him!"

"Your pardon, My Lord, but cannot your power seek him out? Last night when you seized the bard…"

"I was seeing through your eyes and I saw your men fail to slay one man, a man who showed no arcane power. Now go, find him before…No wait, there's no need. He has already promised to come to us. Let him raise his armies. Let him call on the Fae. This keep is strong, built to withstand any force. Let them come. Let them surround us. We will wait them out. In the meantime, I will strip this storyteller of all he knows about the Deep Ones and the Old Gods then use their power against my foes."

"As you wish, my lord. I will call my men in to prepare for a siege. But what of the townsfolk? Conor's army may vent its wrath on them."

"What is that to me? You have your orders. Now go."

By nightfall, there was not a uniformed soldier in the town. Each and every one had been called to the Keep—the unlucky ones on the outside guarding the approaches. The rest inside, to sell their lives dearly should the enemy force an entrance.

Moans and cries of pain came from the Wizard's chamber. "Again, you damned fool. Tell me what you know of the Old Gods."

Seejay could barely speak. The Wizard had not physically touched him but the bard's eyes were blackened and nearly closed. His limbs ached and he bled from every opening of his body. Spitting out a mixture of phlegm and blood, he whispered painfully. "I have told you what tales I know, as they were told to me."

"You lie." A gesture and Seejay twisted in the chair to which he was bound. "The tomes of which you spoke—*The Necronomicon,* the *Book of Eibon, The Ravings of el-Hazred?* How did you come to read them? Where can they be found?"

"Stories, just…made-up stories." Seejay's voice could barely be heard. Blackness approached his mind and whether it was death or unconsciousness he welcomed it.

Maldon paused. He looked through the eyes of the men outside his keep and listened through their ears for signs of battle. There were none. *It is still too early*, he reasoned, *not yet midnight. That is when this knight's power will be greatest. That is the time he will strike.*

"I have had enough of you, storyteller. If you will not tell me what I need to know, your shade will. By the time your friend has marshaled his forces, you will be dead and your bound spirit will have revealed all. But I will give you one chance to earn an easy death. Tell me if you can, to what power would the knight offer a corpse? Of what use to him is a dead man?"

The bard heard the question. It was the only one asked that day to which he truly had an answer. At least, he hoped he did. Then, through what little awareness he had left to him, he heard, "He was my size."

I know that voice, Seejay thought. He forced his eyes open and saw in the doorway a man in guardsman livery. But this man served no master but himself. It was Conor, and he held a bloody sword.

Without another word, Conor stepped forward and swung this sword at Maldon's neck. A gesture of the wizard's hand blocked the swing as if he too held a blade. Another gesture and pain shot through the knight's body.

Conor, however, was not a storyteller. He was a warrior and he had felt pain before. He had been trained to ignore it, to shunt it into a part of his mind not concerned with the battle and worry later about any damage.

"Fight the man, not the weapon," his teachers had told him and so he did, striking again at the wizard. Again Maldon parried, but this time Conor was ready with a riposte, blocking the force of the wizard's blow with his blade.

It was a strange sort of duel, a man with a sword against one without yet both equally armed. The wizard had not been trained to fight, with the power from his hands he had not needed to—until he faced Conor. But that power was enough to hold off the knight who had to defend against more than simple blades. He had the skill to do so, but not the time. Soon real guardsmen would enter. If he turned to face them Maldon would strike him down. If he did not, the guardsmen would.

Conor fought on, waiting for his chance, looking for an opening, listening for the sounds from the hall that would mean his end. He decided to risk all on a single rush, hoping he could endure the pain long enough to thrust his sword through Maldon's chest and that such a blow would kill the wizard. He readied himself then…

"The Fae! They rise! They come!" came a weak but audible cry from the man bound to a chair.

For a second, maybe less, Maldon was distracted; his eyes flickering around the room. It was a second too long. In a fight to the death, less than a second is a lifetime. Conor's blade pierced the wizard's heart, then withdrew and cut deep into his neck. Maldon fell. With a downward stroke, Conor made sure he would not rise again.

As Maldon's head rolled free his spells died. The storm ceased to ignore Nieves and a hard rain fell.

Conor was cutting Seejay free when the lieutenant of the guard came into the chamber.

"Maldon's dead," the officer said, seeing the body on the floor.

"Yes, he is," Conor replied, his sword at the ready. "Have you a problem with that?"

The lieutenant thought back to his last exchange with Maldon. "What is that to me?" the wizard had asked when advised of possible harm to the town. "No, my duty is to Nieves."

"Then you best be about it, Lieutenant. The storm outside is bad and getting worse. You and your men will be needed."

The officer nodded and turned to leave but before he did;

"There wasn't any army of the dead or from Faerie, was there?"

Conor shook his head. "Just another story, Lieutenant."

"One you both told well."

Conor looked at the now-freed Seejay. Smiling as best he could, the bard said, "I surmised your plan and improvised." Wincing as he stood, he added, "And it's a good thing I did or you might not have beaten him. What would you do without me?"

"Without you, I would be in a nice warm inn with a tankard in one hand and a comely wench on my knee. Now I'm bloody, battered, and bruised and likely to be drenched when I leave this place."

"At least the rain will wash away the blood." Looking down at the wizard's body, the bard said, "Damned fool. I tried to tell him, I'm just a storyteller, telling what tales I know."

"You are more than that, Seejay, son of Hender. You are a mighty bard, one who helped defeat a powerful wizard then faced a terrible storm."

The bard thought for a moment. "That's not bad, if I do say so myself."

"Don't worry, Seejay. Sooner or later, you will."

VIOLET EYES

A story of Seejay, Son of Hender

So there we all were, staring at a pile of clothing on the ground while wondering what had become of the woman who had been wearing it. But let me start at the beginning, which is where all good stories should begin. As to whether or not this is a good story—well, I'm telling it, aren't I?

It starts where all good stories should start, in a tavern. This one was in the port of Carney. My friend Conor of Scotia and I had just crossed the Norman Sea and we were seeking lodgings. The Carney Tavern was the obvious choice, for Conor that is. It was a large place and by all accounts comfortable and accommodating. Which meant it was expensive.

"Are you certain, Friend Conor, that you do not know someone in town with whom we can spend the night?"

"You mean for free?"

"Of course. Why spend coin when you don't have to?"

"You did well enough at the festival."

"And I would like to keep what I earned. Is that so bad?"

The knight shook his head, whether at me or the situation I cannot say. "First time here, Seejay."

"Then is there perhaps someplace less costly?"

"There's that." He pointed down the road, toward an inn called "The Skull and Dagger." I tried hard not to be dissuaded by the hanging sign that gave the place its name, the one that showed a skull pierced by a dagger. "I was told by the captain of the ship that ferried us across the sea that it's not a bad place," Conor said. Then, before I could suggest that we try it, he added, "He said that only two of their guests were killed in their beds last week."

We agreed to share a room at the Carney Tavern.

Meals, alas, were not included and the landlord refused my generous offer to tell tales and sing songs in exchange for an evening's repast. It did not matter to him that I was the bard who had helped save the town of Nieves from a terrible wizard, or that I was a storyteller extraordinaire whose fame was known throughout the continent.

"We had a bard in here last year who made us the same offer," the landlord said in a less than friendly tone. "We sent him over to the Skull and Dagger. Not that he wanted to go, mind you. But he just would not shut up. Poor fellow. Damn shame what happened to him. Now then, what were you saying?"

"Nothing, kind sir. Nice place you have here."

So Conor and I ate and drank, and good food and wine it was, if a bit overpriced for my taste, and its taste as well. Now Conor was a man-at-arms, a sword for hire who had helped me in saving Nieves. (Some might say that I helped him, but let those that do tell their own stories.) Now it happened that there were others like Conor at dinner that evening, and soon he and his fellow knights had commandeered the largest table and began to drink and tell tales of their adventures. The more they drank, the wilder the tales grew.

Was I left out of the telling? Yes. Did I mind? No. Why should I give my stories away? Instead, I listened and committed the stories they told to memory. After all, the more stories I know the more I can tell.

Evening had rolled into night and one of the men at the table had just finished a story about two sheep, a tinker, and an angry shepherd. The landlord was giving us the "It's time for bed. I want to close up" look but given that everyone at the table but me was armed and more than slightly drunk he wasn't going to say anything.

Catching Conor's eye, I nodded in the landlord's direction. My friend caught the hint, stood, and announced, "That's the night for me. Tomorrow at dawn I'm off to the west. And you lot?"

"To the continent," said one for all. "Albion's become too peaceful. When kings are holding festivals instead of fighting wars, it's time to leave."

That got my attention. "Sir Ackley." (I honestly did not know if he had been knighted, but no man I knew would deny the title, however honorary or undeserved.) "What's this about a festival?"

"Edward, Duke of Midwinter. He's seeking a bride for his son."

"Are the women of Midwinter that ugly that he can't find one to his liking, or is the son the ugly one?"

Ackley shrugged. "Can't say. Never met any of them. All I know is what I've heard; that all the nobles and wealthy merchants of the dukedom have been invited. Should be quite a crowd."

"A crowd that will need entertaining," Conor suggested.

"Indeed, friend Conor." And with that in my mind, I went up to the room I shared with Conor and two others.

Conor and I said our goodbyes that night. He would be setting out on his quest before dawn. I planned on an early start as well. Having been told by the landlord that Midwinter was some leagues away, I acquired an ass and took the road that pointed north and east. My departure must have been a funny sight, one ass atop another, both of us groaning with the effort of travel. I wish I could have seen myself.

After two days travel with no adventures worth the telling, I arrived at Camber, the capital (and only city) of Midwinter.

Riding up to the castle, I confidently approached the guard of the south gate.

"I am here to entertain the Duke's guests."

The guard looked at me closely. His eyes appraised my face and my clothes. He looked at my ass. (The one with four legs and a tail, not …well, you know.) He did not seem impressed.

"You are expected?" he asked doubtfully.

"Sir," I said loudly as if most offended, "would I have traveled all the way from Nieves if I were not?"

Reluctantly, the guardsman not only let me pass but told me where to go. This was not an unusual occurrence for me since people are always telling me where to go, although generally they direct me to a place much hotter than wherever we are.

Entering the courtyard, I dismounted. After what only could have been a sigh of relief from my less than noble steed, I led it to where I had been directed and soon was face to face with Alfred, a dark-skinned, scrawny scarecrow of a man. He wasn't much to look at but at least he was well dressed. Apparently, Duke Edward did not stint on the quality of his servants' livery.

"You were not invited," he said in a sour voice.

Now I was not about to admit that he was right so in my most pleasant voice I said, "And yet I am here."

"Yes, you are. Very well, what is your name and what do you do?"

Standing as straight as my bulk would allow, I proudly proclaimed, "I am Seejay, son of Hender, and I am a storyteller extraordinaire. Allow me, if you will, to regale you with…"

Alfred's loud sigh interrupted me. "You're a bard." He then looked me up and down. "Can you juggle as well? Tell jokes? Play the fool?"

"All that and I can dance like a monkey."

"Is the ass part of your act?" When I failed to answer he asked again, this time looking straight at me. "Well, is it?"

I pointed to my mount. "Oh, I thought you were talking to him."

The left corner of Alfred's mouth curled just enough to acknowledge the jest but not enough to show any appreciation of it. "No," I told him, "I work alone. Although he does… work under me."

Again the lip curl, this time accompanied by a whispered, "Poor beast." Alfred waved over a page. "Take the ass to the stables, the one with four legs. The other one stays here." Then to me, he said, "You are in luck, Jester, while we have a minstrel, we are in need of a fool. So I suppose you'll have to do. Have you any objection to motley?"

"I don't know, I've never tried it. How does it taste?"

This time not even a lip curl and I hoped that the duke's guests were a more appreciative audience than Alfred.

Another page was summoned to take me to my sleeping quarters. Before he led me away I asked Alfred, "What happened to the fool before me?"

"He made jokes about Duke Edward. Shortly after that, his position became vacant."

Oh damn.

The page led me to a room occupied by an odd-looking man, tall and even thinner than Alfred. Dressed as he was all in black, he looked like a shadow that had somehow lost the man who had cast it. This walking shade was the minstrel Alfred had mentioned. His name was Jook, and I had heard of him. It was said that he had a most marvelous singing voice. Accompanied by only a harp, Jook could hold an entire hall spellbound for hours.

I introduced myself. Jook had not heard of me. Ah well, such is fame, or the lack thereof.

Jook had a high, light voice, almost like a child's. "Five years ago," he told me, "there was a similar festival here, for the same reason. Now it seems that another wife is required."

"What happened to the old one?"

Jook's answer was a shrug. "That is not our concern. We are here to entertain, to amuse the high-born and wealthy. At least the pay is good. The Duke is most generous with other people's money."

"How so?" I asked.

"Attendance is required. If one sends their regrets they soon regret it. And each guest is expected to provide a sizable token of appreciation for being 'invited.' Gold, silver, jewelry. Try not to think about that when you receive payment."

Our conversation was interrupted by Alfred, who knocked on our door then entered without waiting for a "Come in."

"Forgive me, gentlemen," he said in a tone that suggested there was a question mark after the word gentlemen. "I have your assignments for each of the gala nights."

"A gal a night is about all I can handle."

That earned me an appreciative chuckle from Jook. Alfred merely looked at me, shook his head, and said, "I am sorry to hear that. Perhaps the court physician can prescribe something." Alfred then handed us papers telling us in what hall we were to appear and when. He had servants bring in the clothing we were to wear—formal black for Jook (which I thought was the equivalent of gilding gold) and motley for me.

"Jook, I am looking forward to hearing you sing again," Alfred said. "As for you, Jester, please try to be at least somewhat amusing."

Alfred then left, leaving the room in silence that was soon broken by a loud grumbling which turned out to be my stomach reminding me that I had not eaten since morning.

"Which way to the kitchen?" I asked.

As it turned out, it was a long way, made longer by the maze-like hallways of the castle. This, of course, was deliberate, just like the narrow stairways and low-linteled doorways. Invaders are at a disadvantage if they can only climb stairs one at a time, or if they have to bend their necks when entering a room, or if they can't find their way around.

But this did not help a poor, hungry bard find his way to the meat and ale that would restore his strength and prepare him for the rigors of songs and stories designed to entertain the king's guests and, more importantly, induce them to throw some spare coin his way.

Like Moses in the desert, I wandered the halls, asking directions from grim-faced servants. In the two turns of the glass it took me to find the kitchen I passed many a servant and none bore anything close to a smile. Perhaps it was the pressure of preparing for a great event, I told myself. Perhaps, I thought, it was me, an idea I quickly rejected, for who could not like a big, fat, wonderful person like myself. Or perhaps it was because toiling for the wealthy day and night for little or no pay is not its own reward.

But find the kitchen I did and they seemed a happier bunch. And why not? They were warm and well-fed. And generous as well, for when I told them who I was and why I was there, I was soon sitting at a roughly made table with food and drink in front of me, singing for my supper (so to speak) with news from outside the kingdom.

I was halfway through telling the (somewhat exaggerated) tale of the great battle of Nieves when I saw Felicia. She was climbing out of an ash pile. Even with her covered in cinders, I could see there was a beauty about her. It was a beauty she tried hard to conceal, a wise move in a place where the lowly are forever at the whim of those who think themselves high, mighty, and privileged. No one else paid her any attention and she did not smile as the rest did. It did not take me long to reason why.

Felicia was not one of the kitchen staff. She may be working *in* the kitchen but she was not *of* the kitchen. She was, instead, a servant of the servants, her job to tend the ovens and fires, to keep the staff and the food warm, and to clean up after.

A misstep, and Felicia stumbled and fell. As no one else moved to help her, I broke off my story, stood, and reached out my hand.

"Thank you, sir," she said as she took my hand to rise out of the soot and ash.

"Sir?" I asked in mock amazement. "Do I look like a knight? No, my dear, I am merely Seejay, a humble jester here to amuse the guests. And you are?"

She smiled, and her strange violet eyes flashed as she said, "I am called Felicia. Thank you for your help … Sir Seejay." She said this last with muted mockery, turning my joke back on me.

Once standing, Felicia made no effort to clean herself but returned to her work, hauling the garbage out to the hall to be carried away by others like her.

It was a brief but interesting encounter, one that bothered my mind while my hands and eyes were occupied juggling a bowl, a half-eaten leg of mutton, and a very sharp knife for the amusement of the kitchen staff. For this feat, I was rewarded with meat between bread, which I must confess I ate on the journey back to my room so I would not have to share with Jook. The journey back was much shorter than the one there—two flights of stairs and three left turns. It was not until I was licking telltale crumbs from my hand and brushing them from my beard when my mind told me what was bothering it. It was the beautiful Felicia, and the facts that her hands were much too smooth to be engaged in the kind of work she was doing and the dirt on her face was merely *on* her face, and not ingrained in her skin as it should have been.

But by then I was back in my room and soon in bed and asleep. And although in the morning Jook complained of being kept awake by snoring, I must say that I happily slept through it.

The next day was a quiet one, with knights and nobles arriving for the Grand Event. Some of these were rather splendid, dressed as they were in fine clothes and arriving in brightly painted carriages emblazoned with coats of arms. Another carriage sometimes followed, one less ornate and bearing liveried servants. But one carriage or two, there was always a small chest or casket carefully carried and guarded by a man-at-arms. No doubt the tokens of appreciation Jook had mentioned.

Others arrived, minor nobles from the border estates. These were less impressive, their carriages old—the wheels worn, the paint faded, the gold trim (if it was gold) flaking. The men and women, young and old, wore practical clothes, designed for travel and not to impress anyone watching them disembark. Their finery, possibly seasons out of date with current fashion, would be reserved for whatever balls and receptions they would attend. Their tokens of appreciation were not in caskets but in pouches worn on their belts.

But no matter the apparent status of the arrivals, they all had one thing in common—their daughters. They were all young and pretty and dressed in a way designed to display their finer, feminine attributes. And all were well-trained, each of them pausing as they descended their carriages, posing for those watching from the towers and walls.

Now I am usually a happy man, always with a song in my heart and a smile on my face. Watching the arrivals that day, my song was tuneless and my smile fake as I realized that these young women, a few not long out of childhood, were pawns whose tasks were to attract the duke, his son, or a member of the court in hopes of increasing their family's prestige or, in the case of the lesser nobles, possibly rescuing the family fortune.

I was not the only one paying any attention to the new arrivals. There was a young woman who, if she had arrived by carriage dressed in finery, would have been the focus of all attention. But this dark-haired beauty was clad in castoff castle livery and was at work hauling water from the courtyard well into the castle. As she was nothing more than a lowly servant, no one but me paid her any attention. I would not have either, but for a pair of violet eyes.

That evening, I was assigned to work the reception hall, where the duke's guests would gather before the first of many banquets. Afterward, Jook would entertain in the Great Hall where the guests would be formally received and given the opportunity to show their appreciation to Duke Edward in the form of coins or jewels. I had no doubt that the greater their "appreciation" the more notice would be taken of them. I thought of the minor nobles and their small pouches and wished them luck, for they stood little chance against the wealthier lords and knights, unless, of course, they had been blessed with beautiful daughters.

But it was, I reminded myself, not my job to worry about such things. It was mine to bring a small bit of joy into their ordinary lives. So putting on a smile, I went to the reception foyer wearing motley woven in the ducal colors and sporting cap and bells. (I was also in tights, but the less said about them the better. Thanks be to Saint Genesius, patron of clowns and jesters, for long tunics.) Once there, I walked among the guests juggling balls, telling jokes, complimenting the young girls, and making innocently suggestive remarks to the wives.

A gong sounded. The dining hall doors opened and a squire announced that dinner was served. My job, for the moment, was done. When the last of the guests had departed and the doors were closed, I walked around the hall—not through it for I was not worthy, or so I was told—toward the servants' kitchen where my own dinner was waiting.

I was almost there when from behind me I heard, "Very good, Jester." I did not have to turn to know it was Alfred but turn I did. "I particularly liked the jest about the tinker, the donkey, and the shepherd girl. It was just on the proper side of bawdy, suggestive but not enough to offend."

What was this? A rare compliment from this sour scarecrow of a man?

"Thank you, Alfred. I do my best."

A look of dismay appeared on his face. "Oh dear, I hope that wasn't your best." I should have known better. "You'll be in the Great Hall tomorrow night. The court will be present. The duke himself may deign to appear."

"And should I forget myself and tell a joke about His Grace?"

I think Alfred's reply was something like, "Please don't. It is too late to find another jester," but I can't be sure, because just then I was again distracted by a flash of violet.

It was just a glimpse and by candlelight at that, but I would have bet coin that it was Felicia. (And that should tell you how strongly I felt that it was.) But why then was she dressed as a lady's maid?

"Are you all right, Jester? You seem more befuddled than usual."

"I'm fine, Alfred, but tell me, how does one become a lady's maid?"

It was Alfred's turn for befuddlement. "Why would you ask that?"

Having realized that I had asked a question I probably should not have, I quickly covered up. "Well, if playing the fool does not work out I thought perhaps a change of profession."

I watched his face as he pictured me dressed in a, well, dress. Then he let out a small chuckle, then a louder one. Then, still smiling, he said, "Most amusing, and an excellent idea. I will ask if there is something fetching in your size for your performance tomorrow night. Of course, you'll still have to wear the cap and bells."

Alfred then turned and left me. As he chuckled his way down the hall, I thought, *Oh Genesius, what have I done?*

The meal was adequate—cold meat, bread, watered wine, all in portions too small to properly sustain a man of my size. It didn't help that as I ate I wondered and worried, so much so that I barely tasted my second, or was it my third, helping. Not about the dress though. Given what I was being paid I would happily wear anything or nothing. Well, almost nothing, there are some things mortal man was not meant to see. No, I was thinking about Felicia. We had only met once but there was something about her that, I won't say attracted me but rather interested me. At our first meeting she seemed more than a scullery maid and the two times after she seemed it more and more.

After doing some tricks and telling some jokes for the kitchen staff I was off to bed. As I lay down Jook's angelic voice wafted up from the Great Hall and soon I was asleep. And if anyone snored that night I did not hear them.

The next day it was time for the Joust. Knights armed with lances riding their destriers toward each other, risking their lives for prizes and glory and the amusement of the duke and his guests.

During our crossing of the Norman Sea, I had asked Conor about this practice. He simply shook his head and said, "There are many reasons to fight, Friend Seejay. Entertaining the high and mighty is not one of them. It is simply foolishness.'

But there I was. While I was waiting for the clash of armor, the gallops of horses, and the sounds of breaking lances I got my first look at Duke Edward. Alone he rode into the arena to the applause of the crowd. Dismounting his horse, he entered the reviewing stand reserved for him where he was met by his court and its ladies.

Edward was a young-looking, handsome man in his late forties. To his right was a younger man who looked so much like him it had to be his son William. To the Duke's left there sat a youth of sixteen or so. Behind these three were His Grace's ministers, advisers, and favorites. I will admit to being somewhat surprised to see Alfred among them.

Other stands had been erected opposite the duke and at either end of the arena. They were occupied by the duke's guests, the ones who had gathered seeking his favor by offering their daughters.

Trumpets announced the start of the tourney. Knights rode in. Some rode out in triumph. Others walked away in defeat. A few had to be carried off. Whatever the outcome, the crowd cheered.

In between jousts, there was archery, falconry, and duels by men afoot. As time went on, I watched less and less of this and found myself eyeing the crowd. Not the groundlings like me, but those in the stands. It did not take me long to realize that I was looking for a pair of violet eyes.

I did not see her but I had not expected to. There were many in the crowd and most were too far away. But shortly before the last flight of arrows was loosed and the last knight was unhorsed, I positioned myself so that most of those exiting the arena would have to pass by me.

To amuse myself and the departing guests, I sang nonsense songs and juggled the three balls any good clown keeps in a pocket. From time to time, one of those leaving would toss a coin or some other object my way. I would catch it and juggle it along with the balls. Coins and objects of value would find their way to my pocket. Other items would be allowed to drop to the ground.

I must confess that, as sometimes happen, I found myself lost in the flight and dance of the juggling. People passed by. I saw yet did not see them. Objects were thrown my way. I used them then either pocketed or dropped them. This spell I had cast on myself did not break until I heard, "You are quite skilled, Sir Seejay."

It was she, Felicia of the violet eyes. Lady Felicia, I should say, for that was how she was dressed, as one of many ladies in a crowd.

She tossed me something, a weighted scarf, a challenge to my skills. Some stopped to watch as I rose to meet it, causing the scarf to flutter around the balls. Someone else threw a coin. I caught that and pocketed both. The was light applause and the sounds of coins hitting the ground.

"You are quite good, Sir Seejay," Felicia said. "Does it take time to acquire such skill?"

"It does, my lady, but it is worth it."

"If one has the balls for it."

First Alfred and now Felicia, I thought. *With wits like these, they do not need me.*

With that, I noticed the crowd was thinning. With one last flourish, the balls flew high then seemingly disappeared. I bent to pick up the coins from the ground. When I straightened, I was alone.

I returned to my room and emptied my pockets. Coins, an acorn, a toy top, and, of course, the scarf. Its weight was a locket *sans* chain. In the locket was a note—*Tonight. Kitchen. After the Great Hall.*

Suddenly things became clear. My lady of the cinders wanted something of me. It could not have been my body. I've seen myself in a mirror and have no illusions there. My skills then. Whatever it was, I hoped I'd have the balls for it. Especially since I'd be wearing a dress.

I am afraid I must disappoint you who are reading this. There was no dress. When I returned to my room there was a package on which was written, "Could not find one your size. I doubt if there is one your size. These will have to do."

"These" were an outsized pair of pantaloons, again in the Duke's colors. Perhaps later Alfred planned to put me on the battlements in the place of Edward's banner. *Oh well*, I thought, *they're better than a dress and more comfortable than the tights.* I washed myself in the sign of the cross—face, nethers, pits—and took a quick nap. Then I dressed for my command performance.

I was juggling, again. After this afternoon some of the guests requested it. Some of them threw things they expected me to juggle. Alas, no coins this time. When the knives started coming my way, I begged off citing the safety of those behind me. When I said, this those behind me promptly stepped aside. The knives kept coming. Soon I had seven in the air at once and three small nicks on my hands. There might have been more but I was saved by the bell. Well, really a trumpet, one which sounded to announce the arrival of Duke Edward.

One should not be armed when in the presence of the lord of the castle. I gathered my edged props and handed them to the nearest guard. (All but one, I kept the nicest dagger—double-edged blade, leather-wrapped grip, what looked to be a jeweled pommel. If the owner had wanted it back he should not have thrown it at me.)

A page proclaimed, "Presenting His Grace, Edward, Duke of Midwinter."

I waited until Edward sat down. Then, not one to be upstaged by a mere duke, I stepped forward, gave as graceful a bow as my girth would permit, and loudly said,

"Your Grace, on behalf of all assembled, we greet you and thank you for most generous hospitality and a most wonderful festival."

There was a sudden quiet as Edward simply stared at me as if to ask, "Who is this clown?" Behind and to the left of the duke I could see Alfred, his hand over his face, no doubt wondering if he had time to kill me before he fled a well-deserved punishment for having hired me.

Was I worried? Maybe a little. But that night I was a fool and stood on the fool's privilege to say what he liked when he liked. And so I went on.

"Your Grace, it was most gratifying to see you at the joust this afternoon. I had been thinking we would have to wait until this nightfall before you graced us with your presence. Instead, you did so before many knights fell."

I had more planned but was stopped by a noise from the ducal throne. It was laughter, and it was coming from Edward. And since he laughed, so did everyone else. When the room was again still, the duke spoke.

"Most amusing, Sir Fool. Seejay, is it not? Alfred has told me of you. Well, then, Seejay, amuse us some more."

And so I did. I sang songs, I made jokes, I told tales of kings and queens, of Conor and the Mermaid, of Darby and the thrice-drunk ale, and of the world's greatest dumplings. I capped off my performance with a rousing rendition of "Stab Them in the Back" during which everyone, including Duke Edward and, surprisingly, Alfred, joined in the chorus.

When the song was over I heard, "Well done, Sir Fool." I had hoped for a small bag of coins to go with the compliment but then I had already been well paid. "Now if you will allow me, I would like to speak with my guests, and their lovely wives and daughters of course."

There was some mild chuckling at that. So, giving the duke the last laugh, I made my exit to his applause and that of the guests.

It had been one of my finest performances, all the more remarkable because my mind had not entirely been on it. No, even as I juggled, joked, and jested, most of my mind was occupied with figuring out what the violet-eyed Felicia wanted from me.

That time of night the kitchen was mostly dark, lit only by the embers of the fireplace. The staff would be taking their much-deserved rest before waking early so that the morning meal might be served.

But the fire would not be left unattended. Should it go out, there would be no breaking of fasts, and there would be replacements among the kitchen staff. I had no doubt who would be tending the fire.

My eyesight is not what it once was. I am close to needing one of Ptolemy's reading stones and objects at a distance are not as sharp as they once were. It's worse in the dark.

So on entering the kitchen I closed my eyes. There was quiet at first, then the sound of controlled breathing. Hoping I guessed right, I called out, "Lady Felicia."

"I am here, Sir Seejay."

I opened my eyes. They had adjusted to the dark. Seeing her in the corner I asked, "So how was it? Dressed in your servant rags you showed up and said you were to watch the fire tonight, making sure that you did not sound too happy about it. Recognizing you from a few days ago, they happily left you to it."

I couldn't see it but I heard the smile in her voice as she answered, "Something like that."

"And did you find what you were looking for as you went up the backstairs and down the front wearing whatever was appropriate to the occasion, making sure to catch my eye from time to time?"

"Catching your eye, Seejay, was the lady's luck. On seeing your skill, I thought you may prove useful to my task."

"Which is?"

"Justice."

"It is for the duke to mete out justice and for the crowds to cheer. When folk like us do so it is called vengeance and people, if they're lucky, get hanged."

"And still the crowds cheer."

That was true. I'd been to more than one execution and although I never cheered there were times I had given my silent approval.

"Vengeance then. Hot and bloody or cold and sweet?"

"The latter. By choice, I am no killer."

"And when there is no choice?"

"I have a blade and know how to use it."

And if I refuse her, I worried, *will she decide that she has no choice but to ensure my silence? And if she tries, will I have no choice but to use my blade? Oh, Genesius, please guide and protect your most unworthy clown.*

Tell me," I said, adding to myself, *And then I will decide.*

"The purpose of this festival," Felicia said, "is for the prince to choose a wife. It is the second such festival. At the first, my elder sister was chosen. All looked good for my family. But after a year, we stopped hearing from her. My father sent his brother to this very castle to inquire. He never returned. After that, the duke's favor grew cold. My father received word that charges were to be brought against him. What was left of our family fled to Cymru."

"And now another festival, and another bride to be chosen, and for you a chance for what you call justice. Is that right, Felicia?"

A whispered, "Yes," and possibly a nod of her head. (It was still somewhat dark.)

"And what of the young girl who is to be chosen?"

"I care nothing for her or the family that seeks to sell her. My family now lives on a small farm where once they lived on a large estate. I want to restore our fortunes."

"You seek the coin and jewels with which the knights and nobles gifted the duke?"

"I do not seek it. I have found it. It is locked in a chest which is locked in a room above the Great Hall."

"And you know this how?"

"For last week I have been wandering the halls, listening and watching. Servants are invisible, even to other servants."

"Is the room guarded?"

"No, to openly guard something is to announce there is something to guard. And guards themselves can be tempted."

"True. So why do you need me?"

"I mentioned the locks. I thought to force them until I witnessed your skill. Am I correct in guessing that you would have no trouble with them?"

She was correct. In my (much) younger days, I was less than honest. There were mouths to feed and needs must when the devil rides. So I asked the only question I could. "What's in it for me?"

In answer, she took my hand and placed it high up on her warm thigh. My reaction to this proved that I was in no need of the potion Alfred had earlier suggested and made me glad that I was wearing pantaloons rather than tights.

I withdrew my hand as gently as I could. "It is a tempting and generous offer, Lady Felicia. But have you anything more substantial to offer? One can pleasurably spend but one cannot spend pleasure."

Felicia sighed. "I suppose there are enough gold and jewels for the both of us."

"Tomorrow night then, in the Great Hall, during the Grand Presentation when the lucky young lady is chosen."

"Agreed. I will find you and take you to the treasure room."

"I look forward to it, Lady Felicia. *Mae'r moch yn hedfan*," I said in the language of Cymru. "May Don smile on us and Beli's eye not fall upon us."

"Oh …yes … of course."

She stood as we parted. Coming close, she held me tight. "Are you sure you want coin and jewels?"

"Quite sure," I said, breaking the embrace. As I made my way back to my room, one of my many thoughts was, *Beware a woman scorned.*

The next day there was much to think about. I was in the employ of Duke Edward, whose trust I had agreed to betray. If my betrayal was exposed, my reputation, such as it is, would be ruined. Not that that would matter because exposure would likely result in my meeting the duke's former jester. And whatever happened to him would no doubt be considered merciful when compared to my fate. My final tale would be a cautionary one, and mother jesters would frighten their jester children with the story of Seejay's Sin to warn them not to become like me—a traitor to clowns, fools, and jesters everywhere and for all time. And worst of all, when the time came for me to leave this world, Saint Genesius would turn his face away and send his unworthy worshipper to Hell to be tortured by mimes.

Still, there was likely a lot of coin and jewels in that chest, and it was even more likely that none of it had been counted so some of it would not be missed. And did not poor Felicia deserve recompense for what she said her family had endured? Why, the poor child was so desperate that she offered the likes of me her favors if I would only help her.

The more I thought about it, the more I knew what needed to be done, what had to be done. And when I was safely away what tale I would tell of the whole matter. One more performance then—the midday meal where Jook would sing and I would jest—and then I would make my plans, scheme my schemes, and pray to Genesius that I would survive to tell about them.

Night came and with it the Grand Presentation. As it was beginning I dared take a peek. Present were Edward, his son William, and the youth who had stood by their side at the joust. And, as at the joust, His Grace's ministers and advisers stood with them. This time, Alfred was not among them.

The musicians played as fathers, uncles, older brothers, or what have you, led their daughters, nieces, sisters, what have you, into the hall and paraded them around. It reminded me of a cattle auction I had once attended in Iberia or a time in Orleans where the rich completed to see who had the fanciest dog.

I left the show to do what needed to be done. I had considered wearing the garb of the night, dark colors so that I could blend with the shadows. But such dress would only call my actions into question should anyone see me. So I wore full motley (*sans* bells, of course) and proudly walked to my destination while carrying what I would need to pull off my scheme.

Felicia met me at the back stairs. She was in dark, male-style clothing that did nothing to hide her feminine curves. It made me glad I had brought what I had.

"The treasure is in here," she told me.

"Very well. Keep watch as I work this door."

It took but a moment and we were inside. And there, against the far wall, was a rather formidable-looking chest.

I immediately locked the hall door behind me.

"Why did you do that?" Felicia asked.

"Should anyone come by and try the door it will be locked. *And should you decide to use your knife on me once the chest is opened you will be trapped with my corpse*, I thought. Not that it would matter to me at that point.

I handed what I carried to her. "Here, put this on." It was a gown similar to what the young women in the downstairs hall were wearing.

"You expect me to undress? Here?"

"No, I expect you to put this on over what you're wearing," I told her why. She agreed it was a good idea and as she donned the gown I worked the lock. I was finished before she was.

With the chest open, Felicia and I looked down on more wealth than I had ever imagined. No, wait, I lie, but I'm a storyteller so that's what I do best. I had imagined it, it was just that I had never expected to see that much treasure in one place. Too much to carry it all but Felicia was right. There was so much that no one would miss whatever we took.

I produced two plain leather bags, filled them, and tied them tight. When I hid them under my tunic she said, "No, I'll take mine now." So I handed her what she was due saying, "We should go."

I risked turning my back on Felicia as I worked the door, reasoning that she wouldn't put a knife in it until it was unlocked. When I heard the "click," I quickly turned, opened the door, and gestured for her to go first.

"If we're stopped, remember that you're a lady, you're lost, and I'm helping you find your way. When we get downstairs, head straight for the outside. You're young and pretty enough that the guards will let you pass. If you are stopped, claim the vapors or whatever it is you women have."

"I know how to handle men."

"I'm sure you do, as the bishop said to the abbess."

Down the stairs, past the Great Hall, into the foyer. Only the outer doors remained. I hung back and watched as the doormen did their job.

She almost made it. She was just outside when,

"You, Stop!"

It was Alfred. There was no mistaking that sour voice.

Did Felicia stop? Of course not. Would you if you had a bag of stolen treasure on you? No, she ran like the thief she was.

I was ahead of Alfred, closest to the doors. So I was the first to give chase.

"After her, Fool. You others, follow us."

To look at me you would not think me fleet of foot. And mostly you would be right. But that night I had a beautiful girl with violet eyes to die for in front of me and a growing crowd in pursuit behind me. *Genesius be with me. Let this work.*

The saint heard me. The path to Camber turned. For a few seconds, Felicia was out of sight. A few seconds later so was I. When Alfred and the ducal guards, accompanied by Lord William, no less, came up on me they found me staring at a pile of clothing on the ground.

"It was the most amazing thing," I told the crowd, huffing and puffing (only some of which was feigned) as I spoke. "I was so close. I almost had her. I had just reached my hand to take her arm when she laughed and said, 'Not tonight, son of Puck,' and then …" More huffing and puffing. "… there was a bright light and a tinkling of bells. Then she was as bare as a babe. She was beautiful, with wings. And then she was gone. Someone tell me the time. It must be close to midnight."

At that moment, the Camber town bell clanged. *Thank you, Saint Genesius.*

"My Lord, Alfred, noble guardsmen, do you not see what has happened? My Lord, yours and your noble father's fete was visited by one of the fair folk, a great honor to your house. There may be more present so if you will take this poor fool's advice, you should not ignore your guests on this most special night."

It was one of the best lies I had ever told, and not only did they believe me, I could tell by the look of their eyes in the torchlight they could not wait to get back and retell it.

"The jester is right, My Lord," Alfred said. "You should return to your father and your guests. He and I will remain to gather the gown and bring it to the castle. It will make a fine remembrance of tonight's affair."

William agreed and led his father's men back to the gala, leaving Alfred and me alone.

The dark-skinned man would have been invisible in the night but for his torch and his bright formal dress. He held out his torch and examined the fallen gown.

"No glass slippers?" he asked.

"An old story but still a good one," I admitted, "but it's hard to run barefoot."

"Agreed." There was a pause then, "How far do you think she'll go before opening the bag?"

"She'll run until morning, then find a safe place."

"And then she'll want to kill you."

"When she finds I switched her bag for one with the paste jewels and fake coin you gave me, she will definitely want to kill me."

We slowly started walking back to the castle. "What made you suspect her?" Alfred asked.

"The Maid of the Cinders is not the only old story that has been told. That of the wronged family and the desire for justice and vengeance is another one. It did not take me long to realize that the Duke has two sons and that this festival was to choose a wife for his youngest. So when the violet-eyed Felicia spun me her tale I suspected it to be just that, a tale. I confirmed it with the Cymru 'prayer' I recited for her.

"Which was?"

"'The pigs are flying.' It's the only phrase I know in that language. When she didn't react I knew, and so I came to you."

"Why, Seejay, weren't you tempted?"

"Of course, Alfred. But I had taken the duke's coin and although I am far from perfect, I am a man of my word."

"I do not doubt it. And speaking of the duke's coin, may I have the bag the woman thought she was carrying?" Reaching into my tunic, I handed it to him. "And what about the one you filled for yourself. No, never mind. Duke Edward is rich enough that he will not miss it. Besides, you earned it by giving him a story he can tell over and over, that of the night his castle was visited by the fair folk."

We were almost at the castle, so close that we could hear Jook's beautiful voice singing the parting song.

"Alfred, I have to ask. What did Duke Edward do to the fool before me, the one who dared to tell jests about him?"

"Oh, he promoted me."

In the Ruins of Caerleon

When Conor arrived at Caerleon in the land of Cymru he found nothing but the ruins of a fortress and some ancient Roman baths. Not only that, he was alone. His expected brothers-in-arms were either later or were not coming.

"For this I crossed the Norman Sea then left a comfortable tavern in Carney," he said to his horse, a black destrier whose previous owner had for some reason named "Snow."

"I'll wait a bit, Snow, a few days, maybe a week, before deciding what to do. There's an inn not far, near the Husk. Maybe they chose to stay there."

But those were not the instructions. "Meet at the place where it began, near where it ended. Let the circle be complete." Such was the message that had reached him in Sainte-Paul.

So he set up camp against one of the remaining walls, trusting the night to protect him while he slept.

The next day, Conor awakened to the sun and the noise of armored men and horses. He dressed quickly. By the time they emerged from the forest and into the clearing, he was ready.

There were five of them, three mounted, two afoot. Two of the horsemen were knights of the land, their horses and arms similar to Conor's, that is, better cared for than their clothing. One wore muted green and red, the other tan and brown. The third looked wilder, his red hair and beard long in comparison to the others' clean-shaven appearance. A double-headed battle-axe hung from his saddle and a single-head Norse axe at his side. Conor first thought was "Viking" but something about the man said "Alban." Conor wondered if this would be a problem as the people of Scotia had of late been crossing east into what had once been Pictland and was now the Kingdom of Alba.

Of the two afoot, one was a man whose very look cried "danger," whose pale skin contrasted with all that was dark about him. Black hair, black clothing, the sword at his side black-hilted in a black scabbard. On his back was a bow and a quiver of arrows. Conor had no doubt that there was more than one knife hidden in his clothing. He seemed a man whose work was usually done quietly and at night, either for his master or for payment. Idly, Conor pictured a fight between the man in black and the Alban. *Who would win*, he wondered. He couldn't decide and prayed that he would not have to face either.

The final member of the troop was a woman. She was dressed in forest brown robes and, despite being afoot, showed no signs of fatigue. Rather, she walked with a light step and a smile. In her hand was a walking staff. At her side was a sword in a well-worn scabbard. Around her was an aura that Conor had come to recognize. It was one of magic.

Of course, Conor thought, as he considered the nature of his summons. *How else would a message find me when even I did not know where I'd be?* He had suspected it at the time, now he was sure of it.

Conor did not like magic and mistrusted those who used it. The wizard Maldon of Nieves was still fresh in memory. And then there had been the djinn.

No, Conor did not like or trust magic. But he took comfort in his knowledge that, magic or not, a sharp edge always worked if one struck true and in time.

But it was she who had sent the summons. And since Conor had chosen to answer, he decided to put thoughts of death and battle aside.

As the first to arrive the first word fell to him. And so he greeted them as a true knight should—a long knife in his belt, his sword close to hand, and a smile on his face.

"Good morning to all. I am Conor of Tuam, a knight of Scotia, son of Seamus, son of Liam, son of Conor."

The woman answered for all. "Greetings, Sir Conor. It seems yours was either a faster or luckier passage than ours. Our ship ran into storms from Plymouth to Penzance."

"Which is how I lost my horse." The man in black had a Franken accent. "She panicked, broke her restraints, and tried to swim for shore." He gave a gallic shrug, one that accepted that there was nothing one could do about Fate. "*Tant pis pour elle.* But forgive me, Sir Conor. I am called Etienne du Lac." He did not extend his hand but instead gave a slight bow in the courtly manner.

Conor returned the bow. "The pleasure is mine, but please, I am simply Conor. A knight I may be, but I have never been brave enough to trust a king with a blade that close to my neck."

There was polite laughter at this jest, and a loud guffaw from the Alban. He had dismounted and as he came forward with an outstretched hand Conor realized the size of him. Conor was over six feet. The Alban appeared close to seven, maybe a bit more.

Conor met the offered hand with his own. Fingers closed and each man briefly tested the other's strength. When they broke, the Alban said,

"I am Malcolm of Caledonia, but you knew that last, you being from Scotia. From what part of that land are you?"

"Born in Connaught, trained and fought in Ulster."

Malcolm looked darkly at Conor. "Yours and mine are in conflict then. Must we fight?"

Conor shook his head. "Only if you wish. May I suggest daggers at six inches."

The Alban looked strangely at Conor, then his face brightened in a smile. This was followed by another loud laugh." You'll do," he said then he turned to the two knights, who were by now dismounted. Pointing to the one in tan and brown Malcolm said, "That fellow there is Blackheath of Carlisle and the other is Edwin of Baliol. I have no idea where either of those lands are for I just met the lot last night, having stayed at the inn after coming from the north at this fine lady's summons.

At this, the fine lady stepped forward. "Thank you for joining us, Conor. I am Dandrane of Sarras."

As part of his training with the Red Branch, Conor had studied the ancient texts. He knew the name and wondered if it could be the same woman. She was, after all, a mage. He decided not to ask. Besides, it was unknightly to inquire about a woman's age. Instead, he asked, "Do we search for the Grail, or do we seek Avalon?"

Dandrane smiled. "Each must seek the Grail on their own and the Blessed Isle is only for the few and worthy. As to why we are here, in this place, I shall explain when the others arrive." She closed her eyes. "They are close and will arrive later today. We should have our camp and food ready for them."

The expected arrivals did not come that night. Still, the company ate and drank and told tales until it grew dark and it was time for sleep.

Conor took the first watch. He was soon joined by Dandrane, whose approach he sensed rather than heard, for she moved without a sound.

"All quiet?" she asked.

"So far. The horses were excited earlier but have since settled. You don't ride?"

"Horses do not like me for some reason. It may be the magic. But it is no hardship for one such as me."

If Dandrane wanted Conor to ask what that was she was disappointed. Instead,

"You should try Snow. For a warhorse, he seems a gentle soul."

"Your black horse is named Snow?"

"I didn't name him, my lady. But I believe it is bad luck to rename a horse, so the name stands. Besides, what does a horse care what it's called, as long as it's fed, watered, groomed, and well-ridden."

"It is the same with me, especially the last."

A clear invitation. But Conor had learned enough about mages to know how some worked their magic. Providing one with a most intimate part of himself did not seem to be a good idea. But neither was offending a mage. So with a courtly bow that went unseen in the dark, he said, "I enjoy a vigorous ride myself, Lady Dandrane. But perhaps this is neither the time nor the place."

"Well said, Conor of Tuam, well said." He felt rather than saw her smile in the dark and it seemed as if he had passed some sort of test. "I shall leave you to your watch. May you be relieved soon."

As she walked away, still not making a sound, Conor wondered which was the more dangerous, Dandrane or the wizard he had bested in Nieves.

Morning came, as it always does. The Sun had completed half its climb into the sky when there came the sound of more horsemen. The company gathered at their approach, Dandrane at their head, for she had called the gathering, and most of the rest on either side of her, ready to greet the newcomers or defend against them. The only one missing was Etienne, and Conor was sure that the Frank was close, ready to strike from hiding.

A dark-haired man came first, behind him one with no hair at all. Both men were dressed alike, their surcoats and shield bearing the design of three gold crowns on an azure field.

"The first is Robert of Canterbury," Edwin whispered to Conor. "The second is Theobald of York. Do not make fun of his name unless you're willing to cross swords with him. I know them both, but I do not recognize their coats."

"I do," Conor said, adding silently to himself, *and this does not bode well.*

A third man rode out. He had, perhaps, held back until he could make an entrance by arriving alone. He was a young man in his early twenties, tall and wide with deeply tanned skin and yellow hair. He wore the same design as his companions. *There is Roman, Saxon, and Norman about him,* Conor thought. *He has the look of Albion.*

Robert and Theobald held up their horses so that their companion could pass between them. The young man rode up to Dandrane and, without dismounting, loudly announced,

"Greetings, One and All. I am Arthur of Britain."

Of course you are, Conor thought, not in the least impressed.

Neither were the others. If Arthur had expected the company to bend their knees and offer their swords in service, he was disappointed. Instead of homage, there was a pause, then laughter.

But not from all. Dandrane remained silent, as did Conor. As for the rest…

It started with Edwin, a low chuckle of amusement at the overly proud way the young man had made his announcement. Blackheath followed, his laughter somewhat louder. When Malcolm added his great guffaw, it went from man to man, growing until it became a judgment on the youth's pride.

Arthur remained on his horse, which was as pure and gleaming white as anyone claiming the name Arthur could have wished. The young man's face was red with anger and embarrassment. His hand was on his sword, but it appeared to Conor that he was unsure just what to do.

Not so his companions. They had pledged themselves to this man and they would not see him mocked. As one, they loosened their swords in their scabbards.

We should not have laughed, Conor thought as he and the others prepared to meet a charge from the angry horsemen.

The bloody fight which would have left several dead or wounded ended before it began when an arrow buried itself in the ground between the two parties.

"The next is for Arthur," a gallic voice warned. "And you can fight for your dead king."

A moment of hesitation and decision. Then Arthur found his voice. At his, "Hold," Theobald and Robert took their hands from their swords and relaxed their grips on their reins.

As the one who had not laughed, Conor stepped forward.

"Greetings, fellow knights. I am Conor of Scotia." He then introduced the others. "Please join us in peace and fellowship." The three dismounted but remained apart from the others. Addressing the young man, Conor continued,

"You surprised us, good sir. And sometimes such surprise is expressed in … unfortunate ways." Conor paused. The young man nodded as if accepting the apology Conor very carefully had not made. *Either dense or diplomatic*, Conor thought. *Both potential traits of kings.*

Coming forward, Dandrane stood next to Conor. "The name Arthur is a powerful one. So much so that no one who has claimed or contested a crown on this isle has taken it. By what right do you do so?"

Looking the woman in the eye, Arthur said, "By right of birth, my lady. It was the name given me by my father."

"Which one, Uther or Kay?"

"Edwin, that was uncalled for." Dandrane's voice was like a whip.

"Sorry, my lady. It was a poor jest. Apologies to all, and to you, young sir."

Choosing not to acknowledge Edwin, Arthur said, "My mother was Agnes, my father Thomas. It was he who named me, for he believed that I was destined for great things."

"What parent doesn't?" Conor said softly.

Arthur nodded in agreement. "True words. My father did his best to see them come true, educating me in the knightly ways and virtues. When your summons came, my lady, we took it as a sign."

"We?"

"My mother, and Sirs Theobald and Robert who stood in for my father after his passing. And so here we are."

"No offense, but the wearing the colors of the Pendragon is somewhat presumptuous, is it not?"

"It is, Sir Blackheath," Arthur admitted, "but an army must have a banner to rally around." At the sudden silence that seemed to be directed toward him, the young man asked, "That is why we are here, is it not? To reunite the Isle of Albion under one rule, as did the first Arthur."

Conor turned to Dandrane. "Is that so?"

"I do not know," the woman admitted. "I was visited in my sleep by my patron Viviane, who commanded me how and to whom to send the summonses. Beyond that," she paused and again said, "I do not know."

"Then we must discuss it," Conor said, "but not on empty stomachs." He looked up and checked the passage of the sun. "It's past midday. Let's eat and drink."

After the meal, the company, suddenly without direction or purpose, milled around, not sure what to do next. They looked to Dandrane for guidance, but she had none to give. Conor sensed what might be coming—impatience, frustration. Tempers would flare, fights would start, and blood might be spilled. By nightfall, the company would be shattered. By daybreak they would depart, each their own way.

But then—there is nothing like the sound of a blade being drawn from its scabbard to draw attention. Arthur did this. With all eyes on him, he slowly drew a large circle in the ground with the point of his sword. When he was done, he sat and looked up at the others.

"It's not a table," he said calmly, "but it's a start."

The invitation and symbolism were clear. Soon they were sitting in fellowship.

"Why are we here?" Arthur asked, his voice low but heard by all. "The good lady Dandrane does not know, so we are challenged to discern the reason. Surely no one in this party would refuse a challenge." He paused, giving the others a chance to speak.

Malcolm spoke up. "Never was one for thinking. More for drinking and eating, telling tales and bedding wenches, begging the lady's pardon." Dandrane's nod granted this and the Alban went on. "The only challenges I ever faced involved fists and sharp edges. But I'm willing to listen. I've always been good at that."

When no one spoke after Malcolm, Arthur turned toward Etienne. "It was you who fired the arrow, the one which stopped the fight before it started. Thank you for that, Etienne du Lac. Let us leave it where it fell as a reminder not to rush to battle. Tell me, are you any relation to the first Arthur's Lancelot du Lac?"

The knight in black shrugged. "It is possible. But Francia has many lakes," he answered, but neither he nor anyone else missed the young man's mention of "the first Arthur."

"I have an idea." All eyes turned to Conor. "We sit in the shadow of what was Caerleon, said to be King Arthur's seat of government, called by some Camelot or Tintagel. Perhaps all three are the same. Perhaps they were three separate places. But it may be that within the ruins of this place there is something that would point to our purpose in being brought here, something we are meant to find, something that would indicate what we are to do next."

"Something like what?" Robert asked.

"Who can say? Merlin's book of prophecy, pieces of wood from a table meant for a hundred knights, a crown fit for a king." With this, Conor looked at Arthur. "It takes more than a banner to unite a country. Sometimes it takes a symbol."

"Like a sword?" suggested Theobald. "Or rather, *the* sword. You all know of what sword I speak. If we were to find that, whoever it was that drew it from the stones of Caerleon might be considered the true king of Britain."

They thought about this for a long moment, Conor and some others realizing that any old sword taken from the ruins could be said to be "the sword." But the knight from Scotia knew how to test that, or thought he did. *Thrust it in a stone and see if it comes out.*

"That sword was returned to the Lady of the Lake by Bedivere," Dandrane reminded them.

"We have only his word for that," said Robert. "He might not have wanted to admit he kept hold of it."

"Would your patron Viviane be able to answer that, Lady Dandrane?" Conor asked.

"She might, were she so inclined. Perhaps that is why she brought us here."

The conversation turned to "the sword," no one daring to mention any of its names. Was it one sword or two, where had it come from, where did it end up?

Edwin then wanted to know about the first Arthur's scabbard. "Wasn't that important as well?"

"It is said to have protected its wearer from any wound," the second Arthur told him. "And to heal any mortal injury."

"As to the first, yes. Morgana stole it to weaken Arthur before his final battle and, like with so many things, it is said to have wound up in a lake. As to the second, no. For that you need the blood of a grail maiden," Dandrane corrected in a way that suggested that she knew this from experience.

As they talked, evening came then soon night.

"I'll take first watch," Conor said.

"I'll stand it with you," Arthur offered.

The others settled down, the two men took their post, alert for any noises that were not of the night.

"So, what's the story to be, Arthur?" Conor asked as they walked a circle around their camp.

"What do you mean, Conor?"

"You need a better tale 'than my father named me Arthur.'"

"You mean something like 'I am descended from the bastard child of Mordred and Guinevere, whose conception was the true reason for the fall of Camelot'?"

Conor chuckled. "Something like that."

"Robert suggested a tale like that. But if I would be king, I would be an honest one."

"Then you would be the first."

They walked in quiet for a circuit. Then Arthur asked, "You and the Lady Dandrane."

"What about us?"

"Have you two, I mean …"

"Ah, I know what you mean. And no, we have not done more

than talk." Arthur's "Ah" contained more than a hint of wistful relief. Hearing this, Conor said, "Arthur needs his Merlin, and his Guinevere. Dandrane could be both."

"She could. But I would have to keep my eye on du Lac. Still, the lady and I are about the same age."

I suspect she is much older, Conor thought but did not say. *Very much older.*

Morning came, and work began—the exploration of the ruins of Caerleon. It proved to be a disappointment. Time and the weather had not been kind to that which may have been the center of King Arthur's reign. The upper floors had collapsed upon the lower ones, leaving nothing but rubble. In addition, anything useful had already been scavenged by the locals.

"How many dwellings were built from the stones and timbers of Camelot?" Arthur asked of Conor as the two worked side by side carefully searching through debris hoping to find something, anything, that would justify their coming together.

"And how many people now sit in chairs that once bore the names of Lancelot, Gawain, or Claudin?" Conor replied.

"Not Claudin," Dandrane said with unexpected bitterness. "His would have been cushioned."

"Might any of them might have sat in the Siege Perilous," wondered Blackheath.

"Only once," answered Edwin and Robert as one. The company laughed then went on with their seemingly useless task.

They worked until the sun was high, then again after the noon meal, finding nothing more than some battered cups, a few rusty daggers, the hilt of a sword, and twisted metal that could have come from anything. Malcolm created a stir when he discovered a piece of curved wood that could have once been a part of a round table.

"*A* round table," Arthur pointed out. "It is not necessarily *the* Round Table."

"It is if we need it to be," Theobald said.

Neither Dandrane nor the knights were of a kind to easily give up. But evening was approaching, and all agreed it was not safe to search in the dark.

Conor was the last to leave. He had sensed something pulling at him, or rather, his mind. Something that wanted to be found. He slowly picked his way through the rubble, his eyes closed as he moved by feel and memory. He was brought up short when he walked into something hard.

A piece of flooring from above, only vertical and pretending it was a wall. *There are things behind walls*, he thought. He tried but failed tried to move it.

"Need help?"

The knight turned to see Dandrane. Illuminated by Sun's fading rays she looked quite beautiful. *Bewitching*, he thought, reminding himself of her nature. At her suggestion, they got on either side of the flooring and pushed, causing it to fall with a great crash. Behind where it had been, they found nothing but a chair, in back of which was another piece of wall.

"Leave it for tomorrow," Dandrane said. "If we bring it out now, Theobald will insist Arthur sit in it."

"And which would bother you more, my lady? Arthur sitting in it, or refusing to do so?" She had no answer. "Or Arthur's name mysteriously appearing on it while we slept?"

This time she replied. "Arthur's gallantry would have him insist I take it. I'd likely wind up with splinters in my rear."

And you would have no dearth of volunteers to help you pick them out, Conor thought but did not say, *with young Arthur the first in line.*

"We'll leave it then," Conor said, and the two followed the last bit of light out of the ruins and joined the others.

Someone had built a fire in the middle of Arthur's circle, and after they ate, they talked. Or rather, Arthur talked and the rest listened.

"You are right, Edwin, when you say that this isle is, for now, at peace. But for how long? Better to start now in reuniting it. Raise an army here, take Cymru then move east then north, until the whole of Britain is under one flag, one rule."

As Arthur spoke, he spoke of more than conquest. He spoke of justice, of rights for all, of a time when no one in Britain would be sick, poor, afraid, or in need of anything. And as he talked, the men and woman listening to him began to believe that a thing was possible, or at the least, that such a dream was worthy of the effort.

Perhaps, more than one of them thought, *this is why we were brought here, to witness and become part of a new Golden Age, when the flag of the Pendragon would be flown from the Norman Sea to the Shetland Isles.*

Arthur finally finished with, "I have talked much, and it is late, and who knows what tomorrow will bring. But whatever is decided, let us remember the first Arthur's Pentecostal Oath.

"Never cause outrage or do murder. Flee treason. Never be cruel. Always grant mercy to those who ask it and justice to those who deserve it. Give to the poor and protect the weak. Take no part in wrongful battle. Be honorable in all things. Be neither tarnished nor afraid and always give homage to God. This I so swear."

As one, the company replied, "This we so swear."

"It is good," Arthur said. "Now let us set the watch and find sleep. Tomorrow is a new day, with new hope."

But it would not be a new day for all.

A cry in the night just before dawn woke everyone up. Theobald and Robert came from where they had been standing watch. The fire was dying but at a glance from Dandrane it flared up.

The light showed who had screamed. It was Arthur. He had been pierced with an arrow.

The arrow was in his thigh, near his groin. By the time Conor reached the young man, Dandrane and Malcolm were already there. The others quickly followed.

The entire company was familiar with this type of wound.

"If we pull it out," Edwin said, "he will bleed to death."

"And if we don't," added Etienne, "he will still bleed to death but more slowly."

"Who did this?" Robert asked of the moaning Arthur.

"I, I did not see," the young man painfully replied.

A dying king, a wound near the groin. There was but one hope.

"The Dolorous Stroke," Conor said, more to Dandrane than anyone else, "may only be cured by a Grail Maiden."

"Maiden blood can only be shed once, and mine was given many years ago," Dandrane said.

"A girl from the town," Theobald suggested. "There may be time."

"The cost is too dear," Dandrane objected. "I know."

"Whatever the price, it must be paid."

"No, Robert," Arthur said. "No that, not for me." He struggled for breath. "It was but a dream, and most dreams do not last the night. But what a night. We almost…"

For a moment Arthur faded, then he rallied enough to say, "Remember me. Remember the oath." Then he fell silent. Minutes later, with his life's blood spilled on the ground, the man who would have been king was dead.

For a time, the company stood around the body of Arthur. But soon…

"Only one of us is an archer." There was anger in Robert's voice and vengeance in his eyes as he looked at Etienne. "It was your arrow that killed him." Joined by Theobald, he rushed toward the Frank. Etienne stepped back, drew two knives from somewhere on his person, and would have thrown them had not Conor stepped between him and Arthur's two knights.

"Wait," he said. "Do nothing outrageous. Do justice to those who deserve it."

Arthur's words from the night before caused the two to pause, but Conor knew that they would not be held long. He looked at Arthur.

"The arrow that killed him. It stands upright, as if Arthur had been stabbed, not shot. And the one arrow we know Etienne did fire, the one Arthur bade us leave in place, it is gone." They looked to where that arrow had fallen. It was no longer there. "At night, while we slept, someone took that arrow of peace and used it to kill the dream."

"But who?"

"Any one of us, Lady."

"Not Robert or I, Blackheath."

"Why not, Theobald? A dead martyr is better than a live king."

"Peace, good sirs!" Conor's shout quieted them. *For now*, he thought, *but soon they will all turn on each other and truly end the dream.* "Blackheath, while it is possible that one day Theobald and Robert might have decided that a dead Arthur would be more useful than a live one, they would likely have waited until more people had heard of him. Any of us could have killed Arthur. *Especially the one who had good reason*, he thought.

"But who, and how will we know?"

"I have an idea, Malcolm. Last night, Dandrane and I found

something. It was too late and too dark to bring it out but now is the time. Malcolm, can you keep the rest from killing each other while the lady and I retrieve it?"

The Caledonian hefted his axe. "The flat of my axe will put any of them down. If need be, its blade will keep them there."

Conor led Dandrane back to the ruins. On the way, Conor asked, "Did the king have to die so that the land could live?"

"No," Dandrane said vehemently. "How could you think that?"

"The question had to be asked. And if I thought it was so, I would not be walking with you. Such a sacrifice requires a willing offering."

"That is so, Conor." They walked some more before Dandrane asked, "What are you planning?" He told her. "It is a great risk."

"It's the only chance we have."

They went to the chair they had found the night before. As they removed it, they had no way of knowing that behind the remaining upright section of floor was a door. If they had known, had they opened it, all might have been different.

As they carried the chair to where Arthur lay, some of the company moved to help them. "Stay," Conor commanded. When they obeyed, Conor and Dandrane set the chair facing Arthur's body.

"This is a chair of great import," Dandrane said. "I felt it last night, as did Conor of Scotia. It is the sole remaining chair from the time of the first Arthur. And now that it has been placed in front of the king who will never be, let its power be revealed."

Flames burst from the back of the chair. They did not consume the chair but instead flared only briefly before going out. When it did, there was written on it "Siege Perilous."

"All of you know of this chair, the one in which only a pure knight could sit. Percival sat in it and attained the Grail. So did Galahad, and he, too, saw the Cup. Anyone who sat in this and was not worthy died a terrible death."

Conor's eyes looked around the company. "While I do not believe that any of us, save one," here he looked at Dandrane, "is worthy of the Grail, we took King Arthur's Oath last night. It was given to us by and in the presence of the second Arthur. All our knightly sins were thus washed away, and we went to sleep pure knights. We are still pure knights, save for the one who killed Arthur. For him, it is death to occupy the Siege Perilous."

Conor dared not let them think too long. He quickly moved to the chair. "It is my idea, and so I will be the first."

He sat and survived. Standing, he said, "My Lady Dandrane."

"Willingly, Sir Conor, for I am a pure knight."

She sat and survived. Standing, she asked, "Who is next?"

"I will go," Said Etienne, "to satisfy those who might think I am other than a pure knight."

As the Frank walked to the chair, Conor looked at the others. All looked nervous, one more than the rest.

Etienne sat and survived, as did Edwin.

It's time, Conor thought. "Malcolm of Caledonia, pray take the seat."

The large Alban hesitated. He looked at the chair, then at Conor, then at the chair again. There was sweat on his brow when he strode over to Conor. Axe in hand, he said, "I do not think I will, Conor of Scotia. For I do not trust you."

"Do you trust me, Malcolm?"

"Nay, Lady Dandrane, for you stand with him."

Robert then spoke up. "Then Theobald, Blackheath, and I will sit in the chair. And when we are all again standing, then we will know who among us is not a pure knight." He moved toward the chair.

"Hold!" cried Malcolm. They did, but, like the others, put their hands on their weapons. "I killed him, but I had no choice."

"Explain," Conor demanded.

"Arthur's goal was to conquer all of Britain. I believe he could have, including my own country. I could not, would not allow that. So I acted, and hoped to be gone by the time the deed was discovered. I did not expect him to cry out so."

"Why did you not openly challenge him, as befits a true knight?"

"Bah, I am a warrior, not a knight. I do what needs to be done, however I must do it. Besides, he is…was Arthur. No doubt he would have won."

Malcolm paused and weighed his double-bladed battle axe in his hand. "Must we fight, man of Scotia?"

Drawing his sword, Conor said, "We must, Malcolm of Caledonia."

Quicker than thought, the Alban swung his axe. Conor deftly avoided the blow. Another swing, this one downwards so as to cleave Conor's head. Another miss, this one by less than the first.

Conor now had the measure of the man—strength, force, and speed; no subtlety. Again the axe swung, with Malcolm stepping forward in anticipation of Conor moving back.

Instead, Conor ducked under the Alban's blade and thrust with his own. His sword struck home, burying itself in Malcolm's thigh. When he withdrew his sword, blood gushed from the wound.

The large man paled, uttered, "Damn you, Scotian," then closed his eyes and fell dead to the ground.

"It is shame. I liked the man."

It was Etienne who said this. Conor turned and saw the Frank with his bow drawn, ready to fire should Conor fall. Looking around, he saw that the others, even Dandrane, had their swords at the ready. There was no way would Malcolm have survived the day.

"So did I," Conor agreed. "He had a good laugh; made you laugh with him."

"We need to bury Arthur."

No one argued with Theobald, and they spent the rest of the day building a cairn from the rubble and stones of Caerleon. They buried him with his sword and the few objects they had recovered from the ruins. The last thing they added was the arrow that killed him.

On the top of the cairn was a large stone on which they inscribed, "Here lies Arthur, the King Who Never Was."

The sad deed done, they stood around the cairn and, with heads bowed, each prayed in their own way. When they had finished, Edwin pointed his sword at Malcolm's body and asked,

"And what of *that*?"

"Strip it," said Robert. "Burn its clothes and break its weapons. Throw it in the woods for the animals to devour. Let it have no peace in the world after this one."

"No," argued Conor. "That is not the way of the oath we took last night. Yes, he did a foul thing." He looked over at his fallen foe. "But he died in combat and, by his lights, for his country. Maybe an angel is right now claiming his soul. So let us bury him as a man should be, but without words, and without a marker. And from here on, let no one speak his name."

They nodded their agreement. A hole was dug, the Alban was placed in it, covered over, then forgotten.

"There is one more thing before we part," Dandrane said, "so that Arthur's death not be in vain."

She walked over to the circle Arthur had drawn two nights before. It was partly gone, so she renewed it with her sword. Then she took her place outside it, as did the others.

"Let this circle bind us. Let us renew Arthur's vow, today and every year on this day. I, Dandrane of the Grail, now Knight of the Circle, swear to never cause outrage or do murder. Never to flee treason. Never to be cruel. To always grant mercy to those who ask it and justice to those who deserve it. To give to the poor and protect the weak. To take no part in wrongful battle. I swear to be honorable in all things, to be neither tarnished nor afraid, and to always give homage to God."

One by one they took the oath and when the last one had sworn, stood together as Knights of the Circle.

"It is time to depart," Edwin said to Conor and Dandrane after the midday meal. "We have decided to travel together, to tell Arthur's tale and do good in his name. Will you join us?"

"I feel my destiny lies elsewhere," Conor said. "But I will be with you in spirit and yours will be with me."

"I too must decline," Dandrane said. "My life is not my own. I travel where I am bidden and do what I must. But the Circle will always be with me."

Conor and Dandrane stood by the grave of Arthur and watched the company depart. The last they heard from them was Etienne asking, "Tell me, Theobald. Before you lost your hair, was your name simply Theo?"

"You damned Frank, I'll teach you to mock me."

"You don't have to. I already know how."

When the company was out of sight, Conor said, "Nice trick with the chair. That convinced them."

Dandrane looked at Conor strangely. "I thought it was something you had done."

They looked toward the chair. It was gone. Conor turned toward the ruins.

"The ruins of Caerleon," he said. "Camelot that once was." Dandrane said nothing. Both stood silent until the knight pointed out,

"Etienne took … the Alban's horse."

"So?"

"So you have nothing to ride."

Dandrane looked at Conor and said in a certain voice and with a certain look, "Are you sure?"

Oh, what the hell? Conor thought. *What is life without some risk?*

The two spent a pleasant night together and the next day went their own ways.

In the ruins of Caerleon, behind the door about which Conor and Dandrane knew nothing, was the great hall where Arthur the King had once held court. Neither time nor weather had affected this hall, for it stood outside both. In the center of the hall was the Table, around which were one hundred chairs.

The chairs once bore the names of the knights who had sat in them. One by one the names had faded, as, one by one, the knights had died. Before Dandrane's summons and the arrival of the company, only seven chairs were still named.

Bors the Younger, Marrok the Wolf, Bedivere, Dagonet the Jester, Sagamore the Hothead, Bertilak the Green, and Galahad the Pure, whose chair Conor had been allowed to borrow and which had now returned. These were the knights who, in some manner, still lived and served. There was one other chair still named, that of Arthur the King, for while he was not alive neither was he dead.

But on the death of the king who was not to be and the formation of the Knights of the Circle, flames burst from the backs of seven more chairs. The flames did not consume the chairs but instead flared only briefly then went out. When they did, written on those chairs were the names of the Knights of the Circle.

And so the purpose of the summons was achieved. The dream of Camelot would continue, with new knights and new hope.

CAPTURING THE BEAST

After the events at Caerleon, Conor remained in the land of Cymru for a time thinking of his past and future. Before becoming a Knight of the Circle he had been a sword for hire, sometimes fighting for just causes but just as often for the money. Now he felt drawn to a higher purpose. Only…he was not quite sure what that was.

He knew the oath he had spoken. He had said the words and had meant them. He had sworn, among other things, "to be honorable, to be neither tarnished nor afraid."

"A man can but try," Conor said to his horse Snow. But as soon as the words left his mouth, he knew them for what they were, an excuse for failure. Then he remembered something his first teacher, a Celtic monk, had always told him,

"Do your best, young hunter, and let God do the rest."

Wise words, the knight thought. "So I will do my best, and trust in the Lord that it will be good enough," he told his horse. Finding an old Roman road, he traveled east, his destination Londinium.

Conor was two days away from that great, old city. The sun was close to setting behind him when he saw smoke some distance off the road. Riding toward it, he heard sounds of fighting. Urging Snow forward into the woods, he came upon a camp in a clearing. Five wagons were in a circle, one of which was burning and the camp was under attack by what appeared to be bandits.

Two of the camp's defenders were already on the ground. Although the remaining men outnumbered their attackers, most were obviously not trained fighters. Their attackers, however, were and the defenders would have already been overcome but for the fighting skills of one of their number. This one, dressed in forest brown robes, fought ably with a staff, its length keeping fighting knives away while its heft cracked skulls and broke bones. Smiling in recognition, Conor whispered "Dandrane" then shouted, "Onward, Snow," and the black destrier charged.

Conor's approach was not heard over the noise of the battle. It was not until he was almost upon them that the knight let loose a battle cry that startled all the combatants. Then he was in their midst, a wolf among sheep. One of the attackers lost his head to Conor's sword. Another fell to a well-placed thrust. Lady Dandrane struck down yet another with her staff. The camp's defenders then rallied and accounted for two more. The remaining bandits fled toward the road.

Four men on two horses, and neither of the overburdened horses the equal of Snow. Conor was soon in front of them. They turned to find Dandrane behind them.

"How?" asked one of the bandits just before Dandrane's staff knocked him to the ground.

"You can run," Conor told the other three, "but if you do, Snow and I will catch you. And when we do, I will stake you three out in the woods. I will cut your bellies so the smell from your open wounds invites the creatures of the night to come and feast. It will not be an easy death. Or a quick one.

"Or you could surrender and dismount."

The bandits left their horses and raised their hands.

Their hands tied, the bandits were led back to the camp, Conor and Dandrane walking behind them leading the horses.

"You could ride," Conor said.

"Horses don't like me, remember? And as you well know, there's only one thing I like to ride."

Conor smiled at the memory of their last night in Caerleon then asked, "Speaking of your magic, why didn't you use it against these robbers?"

"It's not the kind of magic I do. If it were, I wouldn't need to carry a sword. And before you ask, it's back in one of the wagons."

"At least you're very good with your staff."

"So are you, as I recall."

Conor felt it was time to change the subject. "How did you come to travel with the Rom?"

"How did you know …?"

"That they're of Romany? I've spent some time with them. Now, what about you?"

"I was called to them. There is something … not evil exactly but darkly strange, as if great wrongs have been done." Dandrane turned her head to indicate the woods. "It comes from in there, or will. It is hard to tell at this point. Would you have really staked them out?"

"No, but they did not know that."

When Conor and Dandrane arrived at the Romany camp they saw that the other surviving bandits had been put to work digging graves, both for their fellow robbers and for the dead Rom. They handed over their four captives who joined in the digging.

"It is good you came along, Sir Knight," said one of the Rom. "I am Geofri, leader of this band of entertainers. With your aid and that of the lady Dandrane, there would have been no band to lead. How do you call yourself?"

"I am Conor of Scotia, son of Seamus, and, like Dandrane of Sarras, a Knight of the Circle."

At this, the assembled company fell silent. Except for those watching the prisoners, they gathered around him.

"With respect, Sir Conor," asked a man whose named Conor learned was Condrin, "are you the same Conor of Scotia who helped King Luca and Queen Constance gain their throne?" The question was asked in a tone of awe and wonder.

So the dukedom is now a kingdom, Conor thought. "I am."

Suddenly he was wrapped in Geofri's strong embrace, "Then you are most welcome, Sir Conor, friend of the Rom and now twice friend." He ended the embrace but it appeared that others wanted to greet Conor in the same manner. Geofri forestalled this by saying, "It grows dark. Tomorrow there will be time for introductions, celebrations, and …" He looked at the bandits who were still digging, "… judgment." That there were more graves than dead suggested what that judgment might be. "Now it is time for sleep. Sir Conor, Lady Dandrane, we would offer you the hospitality of one of our vargos, but as you can see we are one short."

"That is okay, Geofri," Dandrane said, "Conor and I are well used to sleeping rough."

Ever the warrior, Conor said, "I'll stand watch. Dandrane, you sleep."

"We'll share the watch," Dandrane insisted. "Do you want the first or the last?"

"Honored guests," Geofri said, "it is our camp and so our watch. We will wake you should there be any trouble. Now enjoy the night and when sleep claims you, may it be deep and untroubled."

Conor tended to Snow then, from his pack, retrieved his bedroll. It was large enough for two and soon he and Dandrane were settled in. The excitement of the fight and chase having passed, they were too tired to do anything but hold one another tight.

It was an hour or two before dawn. Conor had slept soundly, but now he woke to walk the camp's perimeter, check on the guards, and make sure the prisoners were still tightly bound. Satisfied, he returned to Dandrane's arms and was about to drop off when the night was disturbed by the sounds of dreadful howling. It was as if many hounds were all barking and baying at once. He was quickly on foot, the sword which had been by his side now in his hand.

Dandrane and the Rom were likewise awake and alert. The noise was coming from deeper in the woods, seeming to circle the camp from east to west. It grew louder then lessened, leaving the company to hope that whatever was making the growling, yapping, and barking was passing them by. But then the noise increased as if returning.

Conor took charge. "Dandrane, ready what magics you might have. The rest of you, gather what weapons you can and get ready to defend against whatever foul beast or beasts it might be." He turned to the prisoners. "You there, is this your doing? Did one of you summon a demon in hopes of rescue?"

The bandits denied it to a man. Conor believed them. One of their guards said to them, "Whatever it is, if it attacks, we're feeding you to it to buy time for the rest of us."

For the next hour, as the camp remained alert and readied itself for the worst, the howling of what sounded like thirty hounds ebbed and flowed around them, sometimes close, sometimes far.

"What in Macha's name is it?" Conor wondered aloud as his ears followed the terrible noise and his eyes tried to pierce the darkness of the woods.

Dandrane answered him. "I do not know, but I fear that it is the reason I was drawn to this place."

They stood watch until dawn. As the Sun's rays broke over the horizon, the noise ceased as suddenly as it began. They almost relaxed, but the light of the new day fell on the woods, and there, at the edge of the trees, they saw it.

It was large, the size of a bison. Its head and neck were that of a snake, its body like a leopard's. It had the haunches of a lion and the feet of a hind. It looked at them. Its adder's mouth opened and let out the cries they had been hearing all night, that of a pack of baying hounds.

"It has a neck, and necks can come off," Conor said. With sword in hand, he slowly walked toward the fabulous beast, ready to meet its charge. But as he approached, the beast turned and ran back into the woods.

"Well thank the Lord and sing to His Mother," said a woman named Fitrat, "the damned thing is as afraid of us as we were of it."

"It is not a hunter," Dandrane said. "I know it from times past. It is a creature whose fate it is to be ever pursued but never captured. It is the Questing Beast."

But all talk of the beast was put aside as breakfast was served. The prisoners were served first and were given the largest portions, which to Conor did not bode well for their fate. *If they are to leave this earth, they may as well leave with full bellies,* he thought.

As he ate, he took the time to examine the Romany caravans, the night before being too dark and too busy for him to get a good look. As was the Romany custom, the wagons were highly decorated, carved and brightly painted. Geofri had said that the people he led were a troupe of entertainers, and the art on the side of the vargos reflected this. It depicted knife throwers, dancers, fire eaters, musicians, a strong man, and a trick rider. Conor looked from the wagons to the Rom, trying to decide which of the company did what.

After breakfast, he found out how close he came when Geofri made introductions.

"Florin here is our artist. The wagon that was fired was the first she decorated and she was not as skilled as she is now. Now she'll get a chance to redo it." The company laughed at their chief's joke and he went on. "Ana, Dol, and now Josef, the newest of our company, dance and sing to the tunes Zerenity plays. In areas where it is permitted, Sofia reads the Tarot. Adam is our strongman and Fitrat and Vali throw knives at each other. We all work and we all share in what Fate brings us. Sometimes it is good, other times, like last night, it is not."

"But, Geofri," remarked Florin, "did not Mother Fate bring us Conor and Dandrane?"

"Yes, she did, the bittersweet bitch," said Adam. He was an overly large man with facial scars and mismatched eyes. Yet despite his appearance, he seemed a kind and gentle soul. During last night's fight, Conor had observed him subduing his foes rather than killing them. "With one hand she gives and with the other takes."

Geofri stood, his face dark. "Speaking of the bitter, it is time for judgement. Those six men we have tied up and their fellow bandits approached last night as we were setting up camp. At least one set fire to the wagon to distract us, then others attacked. We lost two of our number and had it not been for the Knights of the Circle, we may have lost more. What shall be done with them?"

There was silence. Everyone knew what had to be done but no one wanted to pronounce sentence. It is a hard thing to say now helpless men must die. But though a hard one, there was but one sentence. The men of the company took the bound prisoners into the woods and came back alone. No one asked their fate. No one needed to.

The midday meal, when it came, was a somber one. The Rom decided to remain camped until the next day then set out again for Londinium. "Sir Conor, Lady Dandrane, you are welcome to accompany us. Indeed, you would be doing us a service." Both knights agreed. "Now then, while we are gathered, if you would, Lady Dandrane, tell us of this questing beast.

"Very well," she said. And they gathered around her to hear her story.

Once in the time of Arthur, Dandrane began, before the search for the Grail, there was a young woman, just out of girlhood. Her name, let us say, was Matilla. She was fair of speech and beautiful of face. Her father, Arenet, was rich in worldly goods. And so Matilla was much sought after. But Matilla turned away suitor after suitor. And this was well, for Matilla, although beautiful to look at, was ugly inside. She could not love; instead, she lusted after carnal pleasures.

And the object of her lust was her brother. One night, she went to his chambers. Naked, she crawled into bed with him.

At first, her brother Geres thought he was having the kind of dream young men have. But he awoke in time to prevent his sister from riding his passion. He rejected her, wrapped her in a sheet, and sent her back to her chambers.

Matilla did not take this rejection lightly. In her anger and lust, she vowed to have carnal knowledge of her brother. And in the demons' realm, her vow was heard, and one of their number appeared before her. And this demon, let us call him Belaste, offered to make her wanton desires come true.

"All it will cost you," he hissed at her, "is your maiden's blood, spilled by me in the usual way."

And so, thinking only of incestuous desire, she surrendered herself to him. But the words of demons are much like the honeyed words of any seducer, not to be believed. She was used and abandoned. In the morning, her bruised and beaten body was found by her lady maid.

When asked what had happened, Matilla uttered only one word before falling into a long sleep. "Geres," she said. And so her brother, although blameless, was cast out by their father, chased from his home and lands by a pack of dogs.

How do we know this? Well, demons are wont to brag, and no sin stays secret very long.

The demon's seed took root, and when three-quarters of a year had passed the sleeping beauty died giving birth to a girl. Since then, this chimeric creature had roamed the land. It has long been pursued but never captured.

"That is terrible," Ana said when Dandrane finished her story. "How could that have happened to that innocent child?"

"As Adam said," Dandrane replied, "Fate is a bitch. And not all who are cursed are deserving of it."

"But if the Beast is forever chased, who pursues it?"

"A good question, Vali." Dandrane looked over the company. "But that is another story. Perhaps, Josef, you would care to tell it."

All heads turned toward their company. Josef was a young man, barely past his seventeenth year. He had the pale skin of Albion and not the darker skin of the Rom.

"My grandmother was Romany and taught me the ways. It was from her I heard the stories, all the way back to the theft of the Nail. She told me that our people seek it in much the same way that Arthur's knights sought the Cup. It is a good story, but only that, a story."

"The Cup is real," Dandrane said. "I have touched it and drank from it. So maybe the Nail awaits its finding. But go on, Josef."

The young man paused for a moment. "It was from my bunica that I learned to patter Romany and fake a bosh. When my father died, it was she who urged me to seek out our people, so as to possibly avoid the curse of my father's."

Dandrane nodded. "You are of the Pelinores. I see the king in you. Tell the story of his sin and curse."

"As you said, my lady, it was in the time of Arthur. There were witches and wizards all over the land. Some were good, some bad, some walked in the gray like Mer... Arthur's advisor. Pelinore ruled Anglesey for Arthur, but wait, are you..."

"Yes, I am," Dandrane admitted. "But your story takes place after I left my father's care and went off on my own."

"You fath... King Pelinore had good reasons to dislike witches and wizards, blaming one for his daughter wandering away."

"Not all who wander are lost, or so it said," Dandrane said with a smile. "But that is another story."

"He would not have any magic users in his kingdom. But one day what was thought to be a witch was found near a lake. Pelinore himself came out, not knowing that she was, in fact, a daughter of the Lady who rules all lakes, streams, and rivers of this Isle. He would not listen but instead gave chase with his men and his hounds. For a day, a night, and into the evening of another day she ran and he followed. Who knows how long the chase would go on but for the appearance of the beast child of Matilla.

"The sounds of thirty or so hounds stopped them all. Then the beast appeared. Pelinore's dogs were so frightened that they ran back to his castle. Some of his men did as well.

"'You enjoy the chase so much, King Pelinore,' the lake daughter said, 'then chase that. Yes, from now until it is captured, you and your descendants must forever pursue the beast, a beast which I say now can never be caught.'

"And from that time until now," Josef said, "one member of each generation is cursed to follow the beast in an endless quest. I am the last of the direct line of the Pelinores. I have tried not chasing her, of being where she is not, but she, in turn, finds me and does damage and wreaks terror until I take up the chase once more."

Josef stood and looked at the members of his company. "My time here has been enjoyable, however brief it has been, but I must go and follow my fate and try to do that which cannot be done. Tonight, when we hear the growls and baying, I will pursue it, and the eternal chase will begin again."

Conor, who had stayed silent through both stories, spoke up. "Just wait, young Josef. Lady Dandrane, is there some way to break this geas? Cannot a curse that has been lain can also be lifted."

"The magic of the ladies of the lakes is beyond mine, Conor. The curse must remain until its terms, however impossible, are met."

"And yet our Lord gave to us the power to loose and bind. And if that which is loose can be bound, surely that which is bound may be loosed."

The knight stood. "Something that Josef said nags at me. 'From now until it is captured,' those were the lake daughter's word?" Both Josef and Dandrane said they were. Conor nodded. "I must think about this. I will return for the evening meal. Josef, do nothing until then." And with that, he walked away.

Evening approached. The sun dropped low but had not yet disappeared. Conor, Dandrane, and the Rom gathered around a campfire for the evening meal. Before they did, Conor spent some time talking to Florin.

"Can you do it?" he was heard to ask.

"I think so," she replied. "I'll get to it right away."

Florin was not at the evening meal. When it was over, Geofri addressed the company.

"Whatever happens tonight, tomorrow at dawn we break camp and set out again for Londinium. Sir Conor, Lady Dandrane, I invite you to ride with us. We cannot provide you with anything beyond camp-cooked food, good fellowship, and maybe a bed in a quickly repaired, still smelling of smoke vargo, but you are welcome. Josef, you too are welcome. You are family now, and together we will deal with this beast. Who knows, maybe Sir Conor has a plan to capture the beast. If he succeeds, we can exhibit her and make enough gold for a few new wagons."

They all laughed, except for Josef. Both Conor and Dandrane knew the dilemma he faced. He wanted to stay with his newfound family yet he was cursed to pursue the beast wherever she might lead. If he did not, she would harass and destroy until he again took up the chase.

"I have a plan," Conor announced. "I do not know if it will succeed. It relies heavily on the exact wording of the Pelinore curse and, in part, on Florin's talents."

Florin chose that moment to leave her wagon. There was parchment in her hand that had something drawn on it.

"Are we ready, Florin?"

"Yes, Conor," she replied.

"Good, and thank you. Josef, can the beast be herded like sheep or goat?"

"Usually she just runs and I chase until I tire. But with help, I can try."

Conor nodded. "Tonight then, drive her towards the camp and we will see if we have captured her."

That night, all were on edge. Stories were told, no one listened. Music was played, no one sang. Jokes were told, no one laughed. The company simply waited for the baying, barking, and howling of thirty hounds coming from one throat.

She came around nine, with the campfire high and the moon pouring its light onto the camp. The noise was the same as the night before as it first ran west, then east, then west again, describing an arc around the camp.

Josef stood, as did Adam and Fitrat, who had volunteered to help herd the beast.

"May St. Sara the Kali protect us as she did the Three Marys," Josef prayed as they set out. The chase was on.

There was baying, barking, and howling that again went from

east to west to east and back again. Each time the arc seemed to be smaller until it was clear that it described a pendulum swinging just beyond the far center of the camp.

"It is time, Florin," Conor said. "Lady Dandrane, will you accompany us, for there is power in a trinity."

"Gladly, Sir Conor."

Slowly, the knight, the lady, and the artist walked toward the edge of the camp. When the beast broke into the clearing they stopped, as did the beast, neither moving forward nor back.

"Now," Conor said, and Florin held up what she had drawn. It was a likeness of the beast depicting her snake head, leopard body, lion thighs and buttocks, her hind feet.

"Behold, daughter of Matilla, we have captured you on this canvas. By my authority as a Knight of the Circle and in the name of Arthur, the once and future king, let both curses now end."

Much to the disappointment of all present, there was no great flash of light or loud crash of thunder. No angels came to sign hosannas or demons to swear in anger. Instead, a great howling came from the beast, at first of thirty hounds, then twenty, then ten, then a single voice that merely whimpered as the beast shrank in on itself. What had been a bison shrank to that of a horse, then cow, then a dog. Then it was so small that the grass hide it. Conor thought the beast had disappeared entirely but then came a sound everyone knew—the cry of a newborn babe announcing its arrival to the world.

Dandrane rushed toward the child, picked her up, and cradled her in her arms.

"For unto us a child is born," she quoted, "Unto us, a daughter is given."

By now the company had assembled. To them, Dandrane said, "I sense no evil in this child. There is nothing of her father within her. She is fully human, and in dire need of a wetnurse."

There was a nursing mother among the Rom. The child, who was named Sarah after the saint of the Rom, was given over to her.

"I guess you will not be exhibiting her," Conor said to Geofri.

The Romany chief shook his head. "No, but she's one of us now."

Josef, along with Adam and Fitrat, came from the woods. "I felt a great release. Is it over?"

"Yes," Conor said. "Go with Geofri. He will introduce you to your new sister."

Josef ran off. Dandrane remained. "How did you know that would work?" she asked Conor.

The knight shrugged. "I didn't. But I hoped it would. I'm not a mage, but in dealing with a djinn I've learned that with magic, what is meant is less important than what is actually said. The letter of the spell more than its spirit."

"In other words, you got lucky." Conor laughed at this and Dandrane said, "It's late. Why don't we find our bedroll."

"A good idea. I could use a good night's sleep."

"Who said anything about sleep?"

The Dragon and the Lady

All Conor wanted was a drink. In truth, there was much he wanted—a good fight in a noble cause, a warm bed with warmer company, a place to settle for a time. But as he rode into the free imperial city of Selestat, foremost in his mind was a drink. Wine, ale, even the *uisce* of his native Scotia, as long as it was wet and there was plenty of it.

The knight was tired. He had been on the road for some weeks, not stopping anywhere for longer than a day or two since he left Albion and crossed back over the Norman Sea. *Perhaps,* he thought, *Selestat will offer a respite.* A few weeks with no robbers, strange beasts, or little men with invisible swords. A few weeks of not being a Knight of the Circle. A few weeks as a stranger exploring a new town.

The Bloody Stump seemed oddly named for such a friendly-looking tavern. When Conor walked in and saw the landlord, he understood. He was an older man named Brad, and he was quite adept at drawing and serving ale with the one arm remaining to him. He recognized Conor as a fellow warrior and had a mug waiting for him by the time the knight reached the bar.

"Lost my right arm in one of those damned crusades, don't ask me which one. I don't think anyone's keeping count anyway. They're all the same. I left it somewhere outside of Tyre. Came home with a stump and enough treasure to buy into this place. The other owner is a widow whose husband never came back. And yes, we share everything, if you know what I mean. I tell you, friend Conor, there's a woman who appreciates what a man with a stump can do." He topped off Conor's mug then, with a chuckle, asked, "What brings a knight like you out on a day like this?"

Conor smiled and nodded at the jest. "Nothing, friend Brad. A week's rest, maybe two; just eating, drinking, wandering around seeing the sights. And maybe in the evening sitting down with an old soldier and telling lies about the battles and women we've won and lost."

"Well," Brad said, "Selestat is a place worth exploring. Been around since before the millennium when the Franks decided they were the new Romans. But here I thought you come about the dragon."

Oh Lord, no, Conor thought. *Blessed Arthur and Saint Patrick, make it not so.* Reluctantly, Conor asked, "What dragon?"

"The one over in Andlau, that one that snatched the lady Jacquette from the courtyard of Ste. Richardes's Abbey and flew away. The Baron, her father, is quite upset about it and wants her back. Word is there are the usual rewards—gold, silver, half his barony, and the hand of his daughter. Although what anyone would do with just a hand I don't know." He looked down at his stump. "Although if it came with the arm I could use it, but then the widow might lose interest."

Conor finished his ale and called for another. As Brad drew it, the innkeeper asked, "What else can I get you?"

Conor let out a long and tired sigh. "A room for the night and tomorrow, directions to Andlau."

It was a day's journey from Selestat to Andlau. On the way, Conor apologized to his horse Snow. "Sorry, I know I promised you a rest. Well, maybe after the dragon, assuming there is one and it's still a menace and the baron's daughter has not yet been safely returned. Why do they always go after nobility? Or is it that no one cares *unless* they go after nobility. And how do you fight a dragon? I guess we'll find out."

Conor and Snow arrived at the Baron's keep in the early evening. He was greeted by the guard at the gate with, "I guess you're here about the dragon."

"Yes, if the situation has not been resolved."

"It has not, sir."

This answer caused Conor to inwardly swear. "I am …"

"I'm just the guard. I'll have someone announce you to the baron. And I'll have someone else see to your horse. It's a fine one, sir. What's the name?"

"Snow."

"But it's black."

"I've noticed that, guardsman. Snow was his name when I

acquired him, and it's …"

The guardsman nodded. "… bad luck to rename a horse. We'll take good care of him." He looked Snow over, then did the same to Conor. "You at least look like you stand a chance. The others…"

"There were others? What happened to them?"

"Wandered around, got lost in the hills, did themselves some damage. But no lady and no dragon."

The evening meal was in progress. After identifying himself and storing his arms, Conor was asked to join in.

"We'll talk after," Baron Pascal said.

Baron Pascal was a small man of possibly forty years or a little more. His hair was grey, his features plain. He sat at the table's head with an empty chair to his right, his daughter's place no doubt. Eleven others were seated—family and other members of his household. When Conor hesitated, Pascal said, "Please be seated, Sir Conor. None here are superstitious, although we now believe in dragons."

Other than a monk reading the gospel of the Prodigal aloud, the meal was silent. When it was over, Pascal rose, looked at Conor, and said, "Follow me."

The baron's study was well-appointed. A shelf of books and ledgers, a less than neat desk, and a table on which a map had been laid out. There were chairs set in front of the desk. It was clearly a place for work, not entertainment.

"Please, sit," Pascal said, taking his place behind the desk.

"I have heard of you, Conor of Scotia. Fighter of mages and lover of mermaids. I hope you are here to add dragonslayer to your story."

"I must first find the dragon, my Lord. Once I do, I will slay it if I must, but first I hope to return the lady Jacquette to you."

"Of course. Return my daughter to me and I will reward you handsomely. Return with her and the dragon's head and I will reward you even more handsomely. Your reputation precedes you, Sir Conor. The bards tell your stories." Pascal made a show of looking around his study. "I have no male heirs and Jacquette has no husband or any acceptable suitors. A brave knight with a good reputation could one day find himself a baron."

"If that day ever comes, Lord Pascal, I hope and pray it is far off. But I must first find Lady Jacquette before any other plans are made."

"Of course. I'll have quarters assigned to you. You may use this keep as your base of operations. If there is anything you need, please ask me or Seneschal Roberts."

"There are one or two things, my Lord. First, may I assume that the hills surrounding the town and abbey have been searched, particularly for any caves large enough for a dragon?"

"Yes, they were. We have brave men here in Andlau, both in the town and in my service. All of them joined in the search, despite the chance of encountering the dragon. Of the caves we know about, few were large enough for the dragon as it was described. The ones that were found were entered and searched. Neither my daughter nor a dragon was found, although we did disturb a few bears."

"Are there many bears around Andlau?" Conor asked. "I note that one figures prominently on your coat or arms."

"Yes, there are bears here, Sir Conor. A good many of them. We've learned to live in peace with them. It is said that one guided Ste. Richardes to the spot where the abbey was to be built. What else do you need?"

"A list of those staying at the inns and hostels of Andlau."

Pascal smiled. "You think one of them might be a dragon?"

"I think that just as Andlau has learned to live with bears, someone might have found a way of working with dragons. I have dealt with wizards and it may be that the dragon is being controlled."

Pascal nodded at this. "I did not consider that. It makes me even more glad of your services, Sir Conor. What else?"

"Tomorrow I want to visit the abbey. Can you provide me with an escort?"

"Take that monk with you, the one who was reading at dinner. He's from there. Tell the abbot to send back someone with more than one tone in his voice."

The Abbey of Ste. Richardes was not far. Leaving late in the morning, Conor and his escort, Brother Francis, arrived as the abbey's bells were tolling sext. They were met by the prior, Brother Dennis, at the gatehouse. After the usual pleasantries, the prior dismissed Brother Francis and asked, "How can we help you, Sir Conor?"

"Some refreshment, if it permitted, Prior. Then a place to work, and possibly sleep as I do not know how long I may be here."

"There is room in the guest house," offered Brother Simon, who had accompanied Brother Dennis.

"Very well," the prior said, for some reason visibly annoyed at his attendant. Then, "Anything else, Sir Conor?" he asked in a way that showed the knight that his annoyance was just not with Brother Simon.

"Yes, I understand that a ...dragon flew over your walls, swooped down, and grabbed the lady Jacquette."

"So I have been told. And too many people witnessed this occurrence for me to doubt it."

"So you did not witness this yourself, Prior?"

"No, Sir Conor, I did not. I was busy elsewhere, as I am most days."

Ah, point taken, Conor thought. The prior is a busy man and this dragon business is disrupting his routine.

"Brother Prior, I will need to speak to all those, whether religious or lay, who did witness the occurrence."

"Surely one report is enough."

"If that was so, Prior, the Good Lord would not have given us four gospels." Dennis did not like this remark but could not argue with it. Conor went on to explain, "One person may see something another did not. In addition, I would like a list of all those who live and work at the abbey, as well as any guests, and whether or not they were present when the abduction occurred."

Prior Dennis visible bristled. "That is a lot to demand, Sir Knight. I do not know if ..."

"If you cannot, you cannot. It is just that Baron Pascal expects my investigation to be thorough and I would hate for him to be disappointed."

Conor knew that although the abbey and the city were two separate entities, church and state, each in its own way depended on the other. The prior could no more afford to offend the lord of the land than Pascal could the Church.

The prior gave a quick nod, whether in surrender or dismissal Conor could not tell. He then turned to Brother Simon. "You're his until he leaves. See that he gets what he needs." He then turned on his heels. He did not stomp away but did walk very fast.

"He is a busy man," Simon said, explaining if not excusing his superior's lack of manners and hospitality. "Even more so with Father Abbot unavailable."

"If the abbot sick or away?"

Simon shook his head. "He has been in the church since the dragon came, either praying for the safe deliverance of the lady Jacquette or hiding in case it comes back. Now then, allow me to show you to your quarters, which are larger and more comfortable than our cells, and arrange to have something sent from the kitchen. Then I will see about sending those who saw the abduction to you. Another disruption in the abbey's routine, I'm afraid."

Brother Simon said this last with no little glee and then he was off.

There had been six people in the courtyard when the dragon swooped in. Three were monks, Brothers Paul, Luke, and Tobias. Brother Luke had been working in the abbey herb garden and did not witness the abduction. But he had had the best view of the dragon as it had flown in right over his head. One was a carter who had been making a delivery to the abbey. The fifth was Sister Ursula, a nun who, with her traveling companion, was making a pilgrimage to the city of Rome. Her companion, Sister Anne, was napping when Lady Jacquette was taken, a nap she would forever regret for it caused her to miss seeing a dragon. The sixth witness was Brother Simon.

Questioned separately, all gave much the same story. It was the sixth hour, Nones had just passed and the sun was midway through its descent. The dragon flew in low from the west, just over the abbey walls. With its wings spread and its body aflame with white light, it hovered over the guest house for just a moment. Then it swooped down, gathered Lady Jacquette in its talons, then flew north until it was lost to sight.

"No scales," Brother Luke said, "not like the dragons I've seen in books."

Sister Ursula supported Brother Luke. "It wasn't much like a lizard. More like a great bird."

Brother Tobias was worried about Lady Jacquette. "How could she have survived with that thing all afire like it was. Lady's likely to be roast meat by now."

"He at least had the decency to bless himself after saying this," Conor told Simon as they reviewed the statements. "These agree with what you saw?"

The brother nodded. "I too wondered about the flames and Lady Jacquette's well-being. But the last I saw of her, she did not appear to be burning, nor struggling for that matter. Sir Conor, I thought dragons were supposed to breathe fire, not be fire."

So did I, Conor thought but did not say. *Which means it may not have been a dragon.* He let the thought go. Whichever near-mythical creature it was, he still had to find it.

"Was the lady Jacquette a regular visitor to the Abbey?"

Another nod from Simon. "She came three days a week. She said our chanting soothed her."

"So her schedule was known, and anyone with ill-intent would know where she would be at a certain hour on a certain day."

"Agreed, but how would a dragon know this, or even care?"

It would not, unless it was sent.

"Brother Simon, among the monks, workers, and guests, who was not here when the dragon appeared?"

"All the monks and workers were present or have been accounted for. We do not track the activities of our guests but there was one, a man calling himself Fintan. He said he had business in town."

"Is he here now?"

"No, in fact, he did not return. Sir Conor, do you think …"

"Describe him."

"Tall, thin, somewhat gangly. Pale skin, white hair. When I first saw him, I thought he looked very much like … a large bird."

"Brother Simon, please tell me he left something behind."

"I do not know. I can ask."

"Please do, and please bring back some supper."

"Any progress in finding my daughter?" Baron Pascal asked Conor when the knight reported to him the next day.

"Some, my Lord. I believe that the dragon, if that's what it was, was being directed by another, possibly a wizard."

"Why do you say that?"

"The creature acted out of more than hunger. It flew over several other people before it took Lady Jacquette. That tells me that she was targeted by someone who knew her routine, who knew she would be at the abbey on that particular day. Why he chose her I cannot say. That will have to wait until I ask him."

Pascal leaned forward. "Him?" he asked excitedly. "So you know who it is."

"I know who it might be," Conor answered carefully, not wanting to fully commit himself. "A guest left the abbey early that morning leaving behind his possessions. As of yesterday, he had not returned. He was described as, well, very birdlike, and his name, Fintan, could mean 'white fire.' Witnesses to your daughter's abduction say that the creature was aflame with white light."

"So this Fintan is the one controlling the dragon?"

"Or he is the dragon." To Pascal's bewildered look Conor said, "What better way for such a creature to hide than to look like something, or someone else. Many creatures use protective camouflage. Why not dragons?"

Pascal nodded. "It makes sense. Please tell me that you know where this man, beast, or whatever is."

"I know how to find him, my Lord. As I said, he left his possessions behind. If you have a mage, he can be tracked magically."

The baron chuckled. "Magic, eh. Set a thief to catch a thief. Use magic to find magic." He sighed. "I only wish I did, Sir Conor. You might be enjoying Jacquette's company rather than be searching for her."

"Then maybe a tracking hound?"

Pascal's palm hit his desk hard. "Do you think we did not try that?" he said angrily. "We brought her soiled clothing to Ursa so she could track her by its scent. All she did was wander aimlessly for an hour before retiring to her den."

Ursa, Conor thought, *Latin for bear. Makes sense to give a hound such a name in a land where bears are held in importance.*

"Magic again, my lord. I believe that the lady Jacquette's abductor anticipated a search, which is why he used a flying beast. No scent on the ground to follow. And he possibly uses magic to mask her scent."

"And why would not this apply to Fintan?"

"Maybe it does. Maybe he flew, and forgive me for this, Jacquette beyond our reach. But trying to track Fintan is our best chance. It may be our only chance."

The baron breathed out in a deep sigh of despair. *And why not*, Conor asked himself. *Every day, every hour, every minute that goes by takes his daughter further from him. And his only hope is a wandering knight who may or may not know what he's doing.*

Conor's musing was interrupted by Pascal again slapping the desk. "But it is a chance, Sir Conor, and I thank you for it. All this time wasted searching the hills and you bring hope by just talking to people."

"Your soldiers are trained to act, not ask, my Lord. The others were not trained at all. In my Red Branch training, I was taught that, when there was time, to observe, question, then act."

"Very well, Conor, I will take you to Ursa myself. But first, a drink for luck and a prayer you are correct. And when this is over, however it ends, you and I will talk. My barony needs a man like you and when I am gone, may need you even more."

After their drink, Pascal walked Conor down to the stable area where the knight first stopped to look in on Snow. He had to explain to Pascal that it's bad luck to rename a horse. Then the baron took him to Ursa.

Conor was expecting an Artois, a Bleu de Gascogne, a Tyrolean, or even a Dachshund. What he did not expect …

"That's a bear," he said when he looked into the very large kennel where the large, black beast was lazily looking up at them.

"Of course," Pascal said. "Why else would we call her 'Ursa'?"

"She's your tracker?"

"And a very good one." Pascal opened the kennel door and Ursa slowly got to her feet.

"Come here, Ursa." When the bear had left its kennel, Pascal told Conor, "Show her the clothes and let her sniff them."

Moving slowly so as not to startle the beast, Conor held the clothing in one hand and cautiously offered it to Ursa. As he did so, he wanted nothing more than to be holding his sword in his other hand but decided that would be taken as a sign that he did not trust the baron or the bear.

Ursa sniffed the clothing then looked at Pascal. "Find the one who wore this," he told her. "It is for Jacquette."

It appeared to Conor that the bear understood.

"It, she understands you?"

"Yes," Pascal told the knight. "After the first Ursa showed Ste. Richardes where to build the abbey, the saint prayed that she be gifted with the ability to understand human speech. The Lord heard her prayer and from that day on, Ursa and her descendants know what we are saying."

"And can she speak to us as well?"

"Of course not. She's a bear. Now go with her, and may the Lord, His Mother, and Ste. Richardes guide you both."

Ursa lumbered out of the stable area, then off the grounds. She paused and looked back to make sure Conor was following then walked toward the hills. Conor hoped it would not be a long walk and wondered what he might find at the end of it.

It took more than an hour for Ursa to lead Conor into the hills. Once there, she seemed to know where she was going, walking by several caves to take the knight deeper and deeper up into the trees.

She's a bear, she knows these woods. This confronting thought warred with, *She's a bear, what if she gets hungry and thinks I'm food?* His only reply to that was to wonder if he had to fight a bear could he defeat it, and if so, how would he tell the baron? He decided to stop worrying and simply follow the bear.

Another hour, or maybe two. He had lost track of time. The only break he had was the answer to the age-old question of what a bear did in the woods. Finally though, as day gave way to evening, Ursa stopped and stood on her back feet. Standing, she was much taller than Conor ever imagined. He rethought his question about defeating a bear and prayed he would never have to try.

Ursa let out a low growl then looked up. Conor turned his head and followed her gaze. There, further up the hill on which they were, was a cave opening from which came a soft glowing light. It was not the light of a campfire; that was red and yellow and orange. No, this was light cast by a white flame.

"Good job, Ursa," Conor said. "Thank you." The bear nodded in response. "Now then, do you want to face this dragon with me?"

Ursa gave Conor a look that said, "I have done my job. Now go and do yours." Then she turned and began to lumber back down the mountain. Conor watched her leave. When it was clear that she was not coming back, he began his ascent to the light.

It was further away than it looked. As Conor climbed, he wondered what he would face. *How does one kill a dragon that may not be a dragon?* He had no answer for this, except to remind himself that if it was alive, it could be killed. Then again, so could he.

As Conor climbed he reminded himself not to look down. In doing so, he looked down. *A long way to fall*, he thought. *And I'll probably hit every tree on the way down.* Approaching the mouth of the cave, he drew his sword and entered.

There he found what appeared to be a man. He was tall, thin, and somewhat gangly. He had white hair and pale skin. The light came from him. He was sitting on a large rock facing the cave's mouth. In his hand was what looked like cooked rabbit. At his feet was a half-empty bottle of wine. He looked up at Conor's approach.

The knight prepared himself for an attack, to thrust if the creature charged, to duck and dodge if white flame came his way. He was not prepared for …

"Finally! It took long enough." Then, "You must be hungry after that long climb." They speared another piece of rabbit and offered it to Conor. "Cooked it ourselves," they smiled. "One advantage of our nature."

Lowering his sword but keeping it at the ready, Conor asked, "And just what is your nature, Monsieur Fintan, as I believe you call yourself?"

Fintan stood in greeting. "It was our father who named us that. But first…" The light emanating from his person slowly faded. "Now that someone has found us we don't need that. And yes, we are Fintan, child of the great dragon Ignatius and The Phoenix, who has no other name. And we are neither Monsieur nor Mademoiselle, being both, or neither. It varies according to our mood, circumstance, and company. We are simply Fintan. And you, Sir Knight?

Sensing no immediate threat from Fintan, Conor sheathed his sword. "Forgive me. I am Conor, son of Seamus, Knight of the Circle.

I come in search of the lady Jacquette."

Fintan expelled a long sigh of relief, the air rippling before them as they exhaled. "Negral, Lord of Fire be praised." Seeing a look of hope on Conor's face, Fintan quickly dashed it. "She is not here. But we must explain.

"According to our parents theirs was, despite their differing natures, love at sight and flight. We do not know how they came together but come together they did, many times, according to our father and quite joyously, according to our mother. We are the result of their unions, their only child. We have the size and nature of our father and the appearance and abilities of our mother. He wanted a son; she could only have a daughter. Theirs being a magical as well as a physical joining, it seems they both got their wish."

Having the feeling that Fintan could talk all night and into the day, Conor felt the need to interrupt. "Forgive me, Fintan, but what of the lady Jacquette."

"We are getting to that. Come with us." With Conor following, Fintan turned and walked further into the cave. As it grew darker, they again emitted their white fire to light the way.

"These caves extend into the hills themselves. Most have not been explored which makes it a safe place for this."

Fintan and Conor came to an opening, one twice the size of Baron Pascal's main hall. There before Conor lay a lifetime's wealth— gold, silver, pearls, rich tapestries, rare books, jewels—whatever men yearned for in their dreams of avarice was there.

For a time Conor simply stared and marveled. "I had heard of dragons and their lust for treasure. I never believed it to be true, always wondering what good it did them."

Fintan answered the unasked question. "Dragons have no need of earthly possessions. It is the emotions—pleasure, greed, anger, happiness, and the like—with which these treasures are imbued. Each piece you see before you has history—how and why it was made, the pleasure it gave the maker and receiver, loves won, lives lost, the happiness and heartaches. Dragons feed off this."

"And this is all yours?"

"We have lived many lives, Sir Conor. And acquired wealth in all of them. This is but one hoard of many we have throughout the world.

And it is yours if you help us right a great wrong."

Conor had thought himself beyond amazement. Fintan's offer proved him wrong. He looked at the treasure and thought of all the good it could do for others, and for himself. Then he suppressed these thoughts and desires. He was a Knight of the Circle and he had a mission to complete and a woman to save.

"Thank you, Fintan. But I search for Lady Jacquette and cannot turn away from her."

Fintan nodded. "Then we are on the same path. Let us go back and I will explain."

Fintan picked up a dusty wine bottle. "*Anno Domini* 325 was a good year, maybe not for the Goths but definitely for wine."

At they sat on rocks near the mouth of the cave, Fintan opened the bottle and the two drank. It was not the best wine Conor had ever had but it was the oldest, and as he drank he imagined he felt just a little of what Fintan experienced with each sip.

"Oh my," they exclaimed. "The passion, the romance, the intrigue. This wine was meant to seduce a high-born Roman matron and while it was never opened, bottles like it were, and they succeeded. Several times, in fact, the matron doing things she never conceived of doing. Unfortunately, she did conceive but managed to convince her husband the child was his."

"It is excellent wine," Conor said politely, "but let's speak of Lady Jacquette."

"Yes, let's. Now that you understand our desire, no, our need for treasure, we can tell you how it led us astray. A wizard, one who is called Rasmus, tricked us. Through agents, he caused us to acquire a jeweled pendant. It was imprinted with a spell of compulsion. By the time we realized this we were ensnared, compelled to do his bidding. He called to us, and we had no choice but to go to him. When we did, he told us of Lady Jacquette and ordered us to abduct her. We had no choice but to obey. We visited the Abbey, learned her routine, then took her."

Conor took a long moment to think about what Fintan said. They could have been lying but to what purpose? They had every chance to attack him but had not taken it.

"Why did he want with her?"

"I suppose what any wizard wants with a beautiful woman of noble blood, for some ritual he was planning."

"Was Lady Jacquette harmed during the abduction? By your flame, I mean?"

"A fair question, Sir Conor. No, we have absolute control over ourselves. We felt that there would be less resistance to a fiery dragon."

"Finally, Fintan, where is she and can you take me there?'

"We can tell you where she is. It is some distance away. And while we can take you there we will not. Rasmus still controls me. Were we to arrive with you he could order me to kill you and I would have to obey."

"You could drop me off within a day's journey."

"And he is a wizard who may sense your arrival. And we would have to kill you."

Conor sat, sipped what might have been the oldest wine in the world, and thought of the problem. Up close, he might be able to defeat Fintan. But he doubted if the fire creature would allow him to get that close. He would need arrows or a spear. He had no qualms about killing the dragon phoenix. If they had their mother's nature they would regenerate. They did say that they had lived many lives.

That thought gave Conor an idea. But it was best to make sure.

"Tell me, Fintan. Were you to die, how long before you return to life."

"A matter of hours. Why?'

The knight ignored the question. "And when you are reborn, do you retain your memory and knowledge?"

"Yes. Again, Sir Conor, why. Ahhhh, We see. Do you think that will work?"

"We can but try? So with your permission."

"Let's finish our wine first."

The bottle empty, the two stood. Conor drew his sword. As Fintan spread their arms in acceptance and surrender, the knight thrust his blade through their chest and into their heart.

Then he waited. An hour went by and then another. The Moon had risen and had begun to sink when Fintan's body started to smolder.

Conor stepped back just as the body burst into white-hot flame. It burned for a time then went out on its own leaving behind an egg.

It hatched and from it crawled a naked babe. Conor watched as the child grew from infant to toddler to young person—sometimes male, sometimes female, sometimes both or neither. Soon the Fintan he had known stood before, their body forming clothing around them.

"Damn but that hurt," Fintan said. Then he waved Conor's apology aside. "It had to be done."

"Do you still feel a compulsion to obey Rasmus?"

"We do not feel it but that does not mean it's not still there. Only one way to find out. Are you ready, Sir Conor?"

"Yes." They stepped outside where Fintan assumed their avian form. In something like human speech, they asked, "Can you sit a horse well, Sir Conor."

"Very well."

Fintan lowered themselves. "Then mount up and let us be off."

Conor climbed on their back and held tight as Fintan launched themself into the air and flew east into Germania.

In his long career, first as a member of the Red Branch, then as a sword for hire, and lately, as a Knight of the Circle, Conor had faced wizards and monsters, and merfolk and djinn. Many times he had been afraid, for only a fool does not know fear. But never before had he been terrified. Now, as he flew on the back of the dragon phoenix, he was. As the ground dropped beneath him, so did his stomach and it was all he could do to keep the food and drink he consumed from spewing out. Holding tightly to Fintan, he closed his eyes and prayed to every saint he knew for his ordeal to soon be over.

Fear not, Sir Conor, said a voice in his head that was not his. *We have never lost a passenger yet. As long as our flame burns white, you are safe.*

Conor tried to speak, but the words were trapped in his throat. So he thought back, *And should your flame go out?*

There came a mental chuckle. *Then our fall might kill you. If not, hitting the ground will.*

Conor shut his eyes tighter and continued praying.

Fintan flew through the day and into the late afternoon. Conor calmed a bit and dared open his eyes. From above, the world looked beautiful and he gave thanks to His Creator for the sight. *Still*, he thought, *I would much rather enjoy it on the ground.*

The sun was almost gone when Fintan thought to him. *We are almost there, Sir Conor. Look ahead and to the right.*

An abandoned keep. Parts of its walls were crumbling and there were signs that Nature was trying to reclaim its own. But mostly it was intact.

Shall we land and try to approach by stealth?

No, Conor replied. *If this Rasmus is any kind of a wizard, he knows we're coming. That is, he knows you are coming. He may not be aware of my presence. Land on the top of the keep if it is open to the inside. If may be that we will surprise him.*

Very well. Hold tight. Landings are the roughest part of the trip.

Now close to the enemy, Conor forced his eyes to remain open. He soon regretted doing so for it seemed that Fintan was diving straight down and would crash into the keep. But at the last moment, they pulled up and alighted gracefully, jarring the knight just a bit.

Fintan assumed their human form but kept their flame burning. "Are you okay, Sir Conor?"

"Now that I am on solid ground. Let's go kill a wizard and save a lady."

"And let us hope that your killing us ended whatever hold Rasmus has on us."

"I was trying not to think of that but, yes, let us hope."

"And if he still has control?"

"I plan to kill you quickly and throw your body at him."

"We were afraid of that, Sir Conor."

They began their descent. The stairs were narrow and dark, lit only by what light came from the arrow embrasures. Conor went first, followed by Fintan, who had dulled their light so it would not give them away.

The fourth floor, then the third, then the second. It was on the first, just one above ground level, that they heard voices.

"I am sorry about this, my dear, but Lord Strife will have his victims. It is the price for his gifts of power and the bill is due this very day."

Conor looked through the open doorway. Rasmus's back was to him. The black-haired wizard appeared young, possibly in his thirties. He was facing a table on which was bound a woman dressed in black robes. Her head was tied back, exposing her throat. Rasmus held a knife and was studying its blade as if accessing its sharpness.

"It is finally the day," Conor heard Rasmus say. "And it is almost the hour. As the sun sets, as the light gives way to the dark, I will summon Strife's servant Bar-Bnikul. As I spill your blood it will claim your soul and grant me another decade of youth and power."

Rasmus glanced at a wall whose sole decoration was an inverted pentagram inscribed with words in a demonic script. He looked from this to an open window to the bound woman then back to the pentagram. So intent was he that he did not sense Conor and Fintan come into the room.

It was the woman's eyes that alerted him. As they entered she looked their way. Rasmus followed her eyes and saw them.

"Lower your blade, Wizard," Conor said. "There will no sacrifice today."

"I think not," Rasmus replied. Recognizing Fintan's human form, he gave an order.

"Kill him."

There was a pause. Nothing happened. Fintan smiled, saying to Conor, "I guess it worked." Then to Rasmus, "As you said, I think not."

The view from the window showed the Sun just touching the horizon. "Close enough," Rasmus said and brought his arm down. Conor grabbed his wrist and held it as the two struggled for the knife.

Both men were strong. Conor's strength came from years of training and preparation, Rasmus's from demonic power. The blade hovered just above the woman's throat. All would be lost if it drew just a single drop of blood. The question was, which man would weaken first.

Then Conor remembered a trick once played by a bard. "Fintan," he cried. "Burn him." He did not know if the dragon phoenix could do such a thing but they did not have to. His shout distracted Rasmus. The wizard hesitated and that was enough. Conor twisted Rasmus's wrist and pushed the knife into the wizard's heart.

There was a roar as the portal opened. A large scaly head followed by several tentacles began to emerge. Letting go of the dying Rasmus, Conor drew his sword and cut off the head. The tentacles kept coming.

He dropped his sword. Taking hold of Rasmus he threw him at

the portal. Squirming arms grabbed the wizard but kept coming.

Conor shouted, "I mean it this time, Fintan. Burn them."

Fintan blazed white-hot. Fire shot from their hands and enveloped the tentacles and the wizard. There was a screech of pain never before heard in the world and the headless demon retreated into the portal, dragging with him the inert form of the wizard. The last they heard as the portal closed was a cry for help from the not-yet-dead Rasmus.

Suddenly, there was silence. The wall was bare, the pentagram having disappeared with Rasmus and the demon. The woman had passed out.

"Come, Fintan. Let's wake the lady Jacquette and return her to her father."

"There is just one problem, Sir Conor. This is not the woman we were forced to abduct."

"Are you sure?"

"He's sure," came a voice from the doorway where stood a woman who was tall, blond, and would have been beautiful if not for the evil that showed on her face. "I am Jacquette. That is just some peasant woman no one will miss."

Conor looked a question at Fintan who nodded as Lady Jacquette went on. "Rasmus and I have been corresponding for a year or so. We finally agreed that he would share his power with me and I would share my body with him."

"Then why have Fintan abduct you?"

Jacquette shrugged. "Time was short and it was faster than a carriage." She looked at the bare wall. "And now, thanks to you, I will have his power without having to further endure his ..."

Her speech was cut short by the dagger that suddenly appeared in her chest. It was the dagger that had been meant for the woman on the table. It was the dagger with which Conor had stabbed Rasmus. It had fallen from his body. Conor had picked it up and thrown it to end the evil that was Lady Jacquette.

"Too bad," Conor said flatly. "It seems that we arrived too late to save the baron's daughter."

"It seems so," Fintan agreed. "What will you tell Lord Pascal?"

Conor walked over to where the scaly head of the demon lay.

Picking it up, he put it in a sack. "That I avenged her death and brought back the dragon's head."

"Better its than mine. I suppose you'll be walking back."

Reluctantly, Conor shook his head. "As Jacquette said, it's quicker to fly. When the woman wakes, I'll see her safely to her village. Then you can fly me back and leave me in the hills north of Andlau. I do not think it safe for you to be seen."

"You are right," Fintan said. "And as we promised, the treasure is yours. We have other hoards. But it is a shame that you did not win the hand of the fair maid."

"There is that, but maybe Pascal has a pretty niece."

To Save the Land

Every minute was an hour. Every hour was a day. Every day was a year. And Rasmus, once a favorite of the Lord of Strife, was tortured for more than five hundred days. He had failed his god and he had to pay the price. First, his body broke, then his mind. And through it all, with what was left of his sanity, he realized that he was in a hell of his own making. And that made it all the worse.

"Lord Marshal."

So engrossed in the map of Andlau he was studying, Conor of Scotia, Knight of the Circle, did not hear the guardsman call him. Nor, as he tried to decide how best to distribute the men at his disposal, did he hear him the second time. It was not until the large, black bear in the corner of the room let out a "Garumph," that he lifted his head and saw the young man waiting in attendance.

"Excuse my disturbing you, Lord Marshal," the guardsman said, his attention more on the bear that had come over to sniff him.

"Don't mind Ursa," Conor told the guardsman. "She's harmless." And she was—mostly. Ursa was one of the Bears of Andlau, all of whom were called "Ursa." This one had taken a liking to Conor shortly after he became Lord Marshal. Part companion, part protector, she refused to leave his side except when the knight made it clear that he needed privacy.

"Of course, Lord Marshal," the guardsman said, not quite convinced.

Two years had passed but Conor was still not used to that title. Despite having failed to save Baron Pascal's daughter Jacquette from the clutches of a so-called dragon, the baron, not knowing the true story, had awarded him the title when the knight displayed the head of the "dragon" said to have abducted her.

Conor protested. Pascal insisted. After some thought, the knight decided that maintaining peace and order in the Free City of Andlau was in keeping with his oath as a Knight of the Circle. He was pleased with his job and happy to have found both a purpose and the first place he could truly call "home" since leaving Scotia so many years ago.

And then there was Alyse. She was Baron Pascal's niece and sole heir. It was understood that Conor and she would one day wed and, on the baron's death, become Lord and Lady of Andlau. Neither objected to this arrangement for, while neither was in love with the other, they enjoyed each other's company, both publicly, privately, and very privately. In the meantime, she ran the castle while he protected the town.

"Well, Guardsman, what it is?"

"You're needed at the West Gate, Your Lordship."

Conor sighed. "I've told you lot not to call me 'Your Lordship.' I work for my living same as you. And if there's a disturbance at the West Gate, call Deputy Marshal Adam."

"But Your Lord…" At Conor's glare, the guardsman corrected himself, "Sir Conor, it was Deputy Adam who sent me. He said there was something you have to see."

"Very well." Conor looked down at his map. *That can wait*, he thought, glad for the excuse to get out of the Guards' Command and out on the street.

"Shall I summon your horse, sir?"

"No, it's not far, we can walk. Let Snow enjoy his rest. He's earned it. Ursa, on the other hand, could use the exercise."

Like Conor, his destrier Snow had also been given a new job, one that the stallion greatly enjoyed—siring colts on the baron's mares. The irony that one of Conor's future duties was to sire heirs to the barony did not escape the knight's notice.

Just another war horse doing his job, Conor thought as he followed the young guardsman.

What could it be that Adam can't handle? Conor wondered as he walked toward the West Gate. *I thought that giant could handle everything.*

Mostly Adam could. Conor had first met him when he worked with a troupe of Romany entertainers to "capture" the Questing Beast.

As usual, that adventure had not turned out as anyone expected. Adam was a member of the company, its strongman. The giant's face was heavily scarred with mismatched eyes and Conor suspected that he was not quite human.

Conor and the Rom parted company soon after they arrived in Londinium. They rented theater space in the city and it looked as if they had found a permanent home. For Conor, however, the city was too large, too noisy, and too dirty, and soon he took ship across the Norman Sea for the continent. He never thought to see any of them again.

He had been Lord Marshal for six months when word came to him about a giant causing trouble in the riverside tavern the Lazy Bear. Bears were tolerated in Andlau and roamed the city almost at will. Some of them, like Conor's Ursa, even understood human speech. So many of the inns and taverns affect bearish names.

Entering the Lazy Bear, Conor walked in on a bar fight. It was five against one, with the one more than a match for twice that number. Conor draw his sword and was about to wade in using the flat of its blade when he recognized the solo fighter. He immediately shouted, "Adam, put that man down," adding "gently" for Adam was holding the man over his head. The giant slowly lowered the man to the ground, whereupon the man punched Adam in the stomach, hurting his already sore hand.

"Conor!" Adam shouted, restraining himself from rushing over to the knight for fear that Conor might misunderstand the situation. After all, the knight did have his sword drawn.

Ignoring his friend for the moment, Conor asked loudly, "Who started it?" getting the answers he expected. The five men all pointed to Adam saying, "He did."

Adam pointed back and said, "They did."

Conor looked toward the tavern keeper. The man had almost as many scars as Adam. Behind his bar was a white tabard on which was a red cross. Yet another veteran of the endless crusades.

"Landlord, by the oath you swore to God, what happened here?"

"It was like this, Marshal Conor. The big one there came in for an ale. I gave him a large mug for which he paid double. Then he sat at a table and was drinking it quietly until these five walked in. They started calling him 'a dirty Egyptian' and things like that, asking him if he'd eaten any babies lately. He tried to ignore them but then they started in on, well, the women of his kind. That when he said something about the men of Andlau preferring their bears over their women and asked if that was because they couldn't tell one from the other."

"And is that when the fight started?"

The tavern keeper nodded.

As Lord Marshal, Conor was peacekeeper, magistrate, and, if need be, executioner. His sentences were final, unless one appealed to Baron Pascal. However, the only time that happened, the baron changed the sentence from two days in the Chamber to a week. No one has appealed since.

Having heard the tavern keeper, Conor came to a quick decision, then pronounced sentence. "Very well, the six of you will each pay one-fifth of the damages."

"But that's a fifth too much," complained one of the men.

"Yes, it is. That's for the landlord's trouble and loss of business. And if any of you object, there's room in the Chamber for you. My guardsmen are scheduled for archery practice and need someone to hold the targets."

When all six had reluctantly paid, Conor pointed to Adam. "You, giant, come with me."

On the way back to the castle, Conor asked his friend, "The company broke up?"

Adam nodded. "As they do."

As had happened to him many times, Adam expected that Conor, despite their friendship, would tell him to leave town. He did not expect the knight to offer him the position of Deputy Marshal.

"Adam, I need someone I can trust and someone the people of Andlau will respect and fear."

"Good marshal, bad marshal?"

"Something like that."

The story of Conor and Adam grew in the telling until it was popularly believed that the two had engaged in a day-long fight until Conor, albeit barely, overcame his larger opponent. Neither man affirmed or denied any of the tales told about them.

When Conor, Ursa, and the guardsman arrived at the West Gate, he saw that it was open, Adam standing in front of it, and two other guardsmen keeping back a small but curious crowd.

"What's the story, Deputy?" he asked.

"They are," Adam said.

Conor looked to where Adam pointing. There, standing just outside the gate, were the Fae.

There were three of them, one male, two females, each one tall and slender with a bearing that put any earthly noble to shame. Their hair was long and white and the clothing they wore seemed to be part of their very being rather than something they had donned for the occasion. As Conor looked at them, they seemed to shimmer, as air does over an open flame. It was as if they were only partly in the world of men.

Conor had never met any of the Fae. He had heard of them, of course, and knew the courtesies due them.

Despite their arriving unannounced and uninvited, they were his visitors and so the duties of the host fell to him. He stepped through the gate to meet them.

"Greetings, Most Honored Guests. I am Conor of Scotia, son of Seamus, son of Liam, son of Conor. I am a sworn Knight of the Circle and Lord Marshal of Andlau. Beside me are my deputy Adam of Romany and Ursa, a bear of the city. We bid you welcome. Please, enter freely and in peace."

The male stepped forward. When he spoke, it was like music coming over a lake on a summer's evening. "We thank you for your most kind invitation, Conor of Scotia, Knight of the Circle. But we did not come to this plane for a visit. I am Finarra of the Tuatha de Danann. With me are Saber of the Unseelie Court and Deidre of the Plant Annwn. We are here for help that only you can give."

"I see. May I offer you refreshment, freely and without obligation, while we discuss what the Fae need of me."

They conferred quietly together. When they parted, it was Deidre who spoke in a voice like chimes blown by the wind.

"We thank you, Sir Conor, and accept."

Conor gave orders. "Adam, wine and table and chairs for five." There was a low growl. "And a bowl of ale for Ursa."

Soon they were seated. Food was offered but politely declined but wine, being universal across worlds, was drunk and appreciated. When she put down her cup, Saber's fingers flew. Deidre translated.

"She asks, without meaning offense, if the bear must be present. She is nervous around wild beasts."

Speaking directly to Saber, Conor said, "Ursa had chosen me as her companion and I take delight in her company. Where I go, so does she. Where she is not welcome, neither am I. But rest assured, she means harm only to those who would harm me or mine."

Saber nodded in understanding.

A second pouring was offered but declined. It was time for business.

"How may I help the Fae?" Conor asked.

"Evil has come to the Land, Sir Conor," Finarra said. "An evil that we believe comes from this world."

"What kind of evil?"

"Foul magic, Circle Knight. It steals strength from the Land, leaving lakes dry and ground barren."

"Cannot your magics combat it, Lady Deidre?"

"What you call 'our magic' is a part of our nature," she explained. "It comes from the Land. We cannot fight what destroys it."

"I have no magic. What makes you think I can fight it?"

Saber fingers rapidly signed to Deidre who in their language said, "Slow down. You're going too fast. No, we are guests, strangers here, begging for help. I cannot say that. It is rude and may offend and then …"

Conor did not speak the language of the Fae. But some things go beyond speech.

"Whatever the lady Saber has to say, please say it plainly. I promise to take no offense unless she insults Adam or Ursa. And in that case, I'll have them work things out with her."

More signing, this time slower and somewhat suggestive. Deidre blushed and said, "Saber signs that in another time and place she would not mind 'working things out with Sir Adam.'" At this, Adam blushed as well. "But before that, she said that the magic being used is hateful and destructive and none but humans are capable of such, and so a human must resolve it."

The three Fae waited for Conor's response to this. Finally, the knight said, "I have seen too much and heard much more about the harm done by my fellow men. But I will not say we are the only creatures to behave thus. But that is a matter for long debate and we do not have the time. But none of you have answered my question. What makes you think that I can fight it?"

"Because we were told you could."

Conor looked at Finarra. "By whom?" he asked though he was sure of the answer.

"We first consulted Dandrane of Sarras, who has ties with the People of the Land. She is also of your circle. We asked her for help. Her magic is much like ours and so she suggested you. She said to remind you of the oath you both took."

Conor thought of the words he had spoken in the ruins of Caerleon. Nowhere in those words was a promise to leave behind the life he had established for himself and travel to another land, no, another world, with no promise and maybe little hope of returning. But an oath is more than spoken words, there is a spirit and a meaning behind the words.

What would Arthur do? he asked himself already knowing the answer. *He would take up the quest.*

"Very well," he finally said. "I will go with you." He turned to his deputy.

"Adam, please tell the baron and the lady Alyse that I may be gone for some time. If enough time has passed that it does not seem likely that I will return, or if Ursa returns alone, there is a letter in my chambers."

"I understand, Conor. But I'm sure you'll be back soon. And I'll buy the wine and ale and listen to all the lies you have to tell."

"Let us hope so. Well, Ursa, are you ready for adventure?"

She grunted her assent. Those at the table stood. Adam withdrew. A door appeared halfway between the woods and the town. As Conor and the Fae walked toward it, Ursa fell in by his side. And man and bear entered the Land of Faerie.

How he escaped, Rasmus did not know. Perhaps his god had forgiven him. Not likely, for The Lord of Strife was not a forgiving master.

Possibly Strife or his demons had grown tired of him, or had forgotten him, or had simply decided that further punishment would destroy him, and why waste time torturing a dead soul. And so he was cast out as being of no further use.

But cast out to where? Rasmus did not know. Nor for the first week did he care. He lay there, on the very edge of a forest, mostly unconscious, as his body sought to heal.

Instinctively, his fingers clutched the ground and drew power from it. When he had drawn enough, he woke. Carefully standing, he saw that where he lay was now a brown, dead spot.

Looking around, he asked himself, Where am I? *He did not know. It was not his world and all he could tell about it was that the power he had taken from it was sweeter and stronger than any he had ever known.* If I take enough of it, I might be able to open a portal to my world. Or, if I become strong enough, I might be able to make this my world. We shall see.

So Rasmus, a wizard from the Earthly plane, left the woods of Faerie and found a nearby cave. Hidden from view, he fed from the Land and grew strong.

Stepping through the door, Conor and Ursa looked upon the world of Faerie. Ahead of them was a forest somewhat like the one outside Andlau, only darker. Where the woods of what Conor had come to regard as "home" were welcoming, this was forbidding. No afternoon meals with your family in there, no late-night trysts with a special someone. No, these woods were not entered lightly, and then only for a serious purpose.

He looked up. The sky was the same, assuming this sun rose in the east and set in the west. He sniffed. The air was different—not better or worse, just different. Just as one meal, or one book, or one lover is different from another but still enjoyable, so did this world of Faerie seem to Conor.

"Now what?" he asked the three who had brought him through who now seemed more solid than they had near Andlau.

"Ask them," Finarra said, indicating that Conor should turn.

The door was gone. *Not forever,* the knight hoped. *I do not want to be trapped here.* Where the door had been stood two more of the Fae, a male and female. Between them was a creature from Hell.

Doglike and clearly male, it was as tall as a pony and black as the night. It was a shadow given legs and teeth. It seemed a beast bred from dark magic.

Before anyone could act, the creature growled once and approached Conor. Ursa moved between the two of them and growled back.

The beast barked. Ursa roared. He came close and sniffed. She roared again and swatted at him. He backed off but just a bit. Then, as if of one mind, they ran off and began to play—wrestling, chasing, nipping, and mock fighting.

"I see Pike has made a friend," said the woman Fae who introduced herself as Roisin. "Pike is a barghest and is usually not very sociable." To Conor, her voice was like gentle waves. "And your bear is called?"

"Ursa, and she is her own bear, one who has chosen me as a companion. Now, please show me the problem."

Roisin deferred to the Fae accompanying her. He was somewhat smaller. With reddish hair rather than white, he seemed younger than the others, if age was such a thing in Faerie.

"This is Drogo. He will show you."

Surprisingly for his apparent age, Drogo's voice was deep, like thunder in the distance.

"Come with me," he said without greeting. Leaving Pike and Ursa to their play, Drogo led him partway around the dark forest to where the grass of the field had turned brown. Looking past that, Conor saw merely dirt where the dead grass had blown away. "I see the woods are not affected."

"The woods are the woods," Drogo rumbled. "I doubt if anything can affect them save the end of our world. And I suspect that they will still be there when a new one is born."

"How long has it been like this?"

"A fortnight, maybe two. And it seems to grow wider every week."

Conor walked to the edge of the devastation, knelt at its edge, then felt and smelled the ground.

It felt like dead grass and earth. But there was an odor about it that Conor knew well. It was the stink of sorcery and dark magic.

Damn, another wizard, he thought. *Well, they can be killed like any other man. If man it is.*

When he returned the rest of the Fae he asked, "How far does this extend? Can you show me on a map?"

"What is a map?" Diedre asked. None of the others seem to know either.

That was a question I did not expect. "It is a drawing of the land showing where things are."

The Fae shook their heads. "We do not need pictures for that," Roisin explained. "We know the Land and it knows us. We always know where things are."

Except for an earth-destroying wizard.

Conor knew what question he had to ask next. He did not want to ask it. Memories of a long flight on the back of a phoenix-dragon hybrid came back to him. He really did not want to ask the question.

He reminded himself of the words of his oath. "Neither tarnished nor afraid." Sighing, he asked,

"What creatures have you that can fly?"

A mount was obtained for the knight. She was a sparkling white steed with wings as wide as she was long. She wore neither saddle nor bridle, and she did not have a rider.

"She is Ariel," Deidre told him, "and she will serve you well." Sensing his hesitation, she said, "You are a paladin, she is your steed. You will do well."

I can do this, Conor told himself and mounted himself on the back of the pegasus, his feet beneath her wings. Not knowing the Fae command, he said, "Let's fly," and she took off, leaving the Fae, Ursa, and Pike behind.

This time it was different. Instead of being a passenger holding for dear life on the back of a phoenix dragon, this time Conor was a partner in the flight. He knew how to sit a horse and he soon discovered that it was no different in the air than on the ground. Rider and mount worked as one and Conor became lost in the joy of flying.

But not for long. He quickly remembered his responsibility and flew toward and over the area brought to ruin by the evil magic.

There, the dark woods. To its left was the area he had seen before. From his view on high, he saw what he had hoped to see—except where it came into contact with the woods, the devastation grew outwards in a circle, if "grew" was the right word for empty ponds, dry lakes, and dead earth.

And like a spider in her web, the evil I seek will no doubt be at the center.

Conor thought to land and to confront the wizard of whatever the cause. He almost gave the command, sure that Ariel would obey, but was not sure what landing in a circle where all trace of Faerie's magic was gone would do to the beast. Instead, he directed her home.

As he flew back, he looked past where the Fae were waiting for him. In the distance, about thrice as far as Andlau would be from its woods, was a small village. No, not even a village, just a simple gathering of dwelling places for people living a simpler life.

He had no sooner dismounted than the Fae rushed over to him.

"Did you find it, the source of evil?" Roisin asked excitedly.

At first, Conor did not answer her. Instead, he hugged and stroked Ariel and thanked her for her service. He returned her to Drogo and only then addressed the Fae.

"I have indeed found the source and now I go to confront it. As in all things, I will either destroy it or it will destroy me, or both. If I manage to free what was taken, the sudden release of the Land's magic may be too much for me."

"And if you fail?" Saber signed, "and the evil remains."

It was a question that had to be asked. "Then pray to whatever god you have, for in that case I do not think even fire from above will destroy it. But if I fall, however I do, please send word back to my world."

"We will," Deidre assured him.

"And now," Conor said, "it is time." As he started toward the center of ruin, Ursa came to his side and would have gone with him.

"No, my friend, you may be needed here. If there is a blast, wait until it's safe then come find me, or what's left of me. Make sure they send me back. As for you, stay where you're the happiest. You understand, don't you."

Ursa was a bear of Andlau. Of course, she did. To demonstrate this understanding she rose on her back legs and embraced her friend. Man and bear hugged, then the man went off alone.

Conor skirted the woods, on the still grassy strip just on the edge. Worried that whatever was draining power from the Land might do the same to him, he wanted to delay stepping onto the bare ground until he had to.

Despite the sun barely moving in the sky, it felt to Conor that he had walked for about a glass and a half. *Time must move differently here than at home.* As he thought this, a chill he could not explain ran through his body.

Soon the woods curved so that he had to step off the grass. He braced himself but felt nothing. *I'm not a part of the Land, so maybe it cannot affect me*, he thought and held on to this belief as he looked for the cave he had seen from above and that he had identified as the magical center.

He found it. Nothing but death surrounded it. Dry lakebeds, rocky soil. No, not even soil, just dirt. Nearby trees were bare and crumbling. Bones of animals were scattered all around. No birds, no insects, no sounds at all. Except …

It was a low moaning; one he had heard many times before. It was of a beast in pain, one that had given up on life and now hoped for death. It was coming from the cave. He drew his sword and entered.

The only light was from the sun shining into the cave. Still, it was enough to see. And what he saw and smelled disgusted him and almost caused him to lose what little was in his stomach.

It was a large, bloated caricature of a man that seemed to have expanded into monstrous proportions. Conor had seen obese men before, but this went beyond his experience. It was a cautionary fable grown large and looked very much like the overinflated bladder of a giant sheep.

Still, the thing before was unmistakably a man and, worse yet, one he recognized.

"Rasmus," Conor said, "what brings you to such a sorry state? Did the demon whom you failed do this to you?"

Rasmus ceased his painful moaning to answer. "Did … this … myself. Needed strength … drew from land … never … felt such power … intoxicating, almost sexual … did not want to stop … then could not stop. Wait … I know you … Conor … the one who … should damn you but I damned myself. Help me as you once condemned me."

"If it were just you, Wizard, I would leave you to your fate. But to save the Land it seems that I must save you. Or, at least, stop your suffering."

Conor thought again of an extended bladder and what happens when one is stuck with a pin. It was, he decided, the only option. At best, the magic inside Rasmus would be released. At worse, it would kill him, and at least no further damage would be done. At *the* worst, it would kill them both.

Conor, son of Seamus and Knight of the Circle, had never expected to die in bed. He always believed he would die in battle, fighting for a noble cause. *This*, he told himself, *was not what I expected.*

With a sigh, he said one last prayer, confident that even in this world the God of all could hear him. Then he thrust his sword into the belly of the man before him.

There was a sound of thunder as the magic was freed. Like water released by the breaking of a dam, or lava from a volcano, the energy of the blast was forced out of the mouth of the cave. Conor felt himself flying with it. As the cave walls shattered, he was struck by flying rock and dead earth. Then he knew no more.

He was awakened by the feel of a rough tongue on his cheek. *How much did I have to drink and what does she look like?* was his first thought. Then he opened his eyes and looked into a face from Hell.

"I think he's awake," came a voice he knew. A voice like low thunder. Drogo.

The face pulled back. Pike the barghest. A familiar growl. Ursa. Then he was …

"Thank the Lady, you are alive," he heard Deidre say. "We began searching as a sound of fury came from the direction you traveled. It was your bear who found you, with Pike at her side all the time."

Helped by Finarra and Saber, Conor sat up. "You should not be here," he said in a whisper. "It's not … safe."

"It is," Finarra assured him, "thanks to you. The devastation is still here but beneath it, we can feel the Land again. It will regrow."

"And the wizard Rasmus?"

"We found no one else."

"Call his name. Call for Rasmus. If he is alive he must be found."

The Fae called for him but there was no answer. "He must be dead, blown apart," Roisin offered.

"Let us hope so," Conor said, then passed out again.

Conor was taken to the village where he was cared for. Ursa never left his side, and Pike never left hers. A week passed before he was deemed healed and ready to return to his world.

Accompanied by the Fae, Conor walked to the door from Faerie. Signing, Saber spoke for all.

"Sir Conor, we thank you for the service you have given us and name you Paladin of the Fae. And while we can never give back what you have lost, know that if you ever call to us from a faerie ring, we will answer."

What have I lost? Conor wondered. Then he looked at the slow-moving sun and feared he knew the answer.

"Ready to go home, Ursa?" he asked. The bear looked first at Pike, then at him. Her face said it all.

"I see," Conor said in understanding. "There is no denying love. Be happy, my friend."

Ursa stood and, as before, embraced Conor. After they hugged, she went to stand by Pike's side.

To Finarra, Conor said, "I wonder what the cubs are going to look like." Then, alone, he stepped back into his world.

It was evening when Conor emerged just outside the Forest of Andlau. The weather had changed. Judging from the trees, he observed, so had the season.

How long was I gone? He wondered, fully realizing Saber's words. *Well, I'll soon learn.*

At first, the guardsman at the gate did not recognize him. When he did, when he was finally convinced that it was indeed Lord Marshal Conor standing before him, he sent his partner to alert the baron.

"The baron and his lady will want to see you," the guardsman said.

So, Pascal has remarried, but the thought rang hollow in Conor's mind.

Men-at-arms clad in baronial livery arrived to escort Conor to the manor. There he was taken to the Great Hall where he found, sitting side by side, the baron and his lady—Adam and Alyse.

The awkward silence was finally broken by Alyse. "Conor, we thought you dead. It's been more than a year since you left for Faerie and in that time, Adam and I found a love that you and I did not share. When my uncle died, we married and …" she rubbed her stomach, indicating the heir already on the way. "What of your ursa?"

"She too found love."

"I found your note," Adam said. "And the cave of treasure. Do you wish it back?"

"Just enough to get by. Use the rest of the treasure well."

"A new Lord Marshal had been appointed but you are, of course, welcome to stay." Adam offered.

"Thank you, my friend, but there is no longer anything in Andlau for me. If you would have someone gather what possessions of mine remain, I will leave in the morning. Is Snow …?

Adam shook his head. "We will find you a mount, one suitable for a Knight of the Circle."

By first light, Conor was gone. He had no wish for sad goodbyes. As he rode east, Saber's words came back to him. "We can never give back what you have lost."

I have lost everything, he thought. *But what is lost can be found, or replaced. Maybe what I need is a small house in a small town in a small kingdom, where I can just be a man and not knight or hero.*

He patted his horse, a white stallion to which he had just given a name. "Let's find such a place, Midnight."

Rasmus awoke in a dark forest. Someone was someone calling his name. The knight who twice killed me, he thought and so did not answer. Instead, he simply marveled at his escape from his own greed and foolishness and gave himself time to heal—the natural way. He was done forever with the darker side of magic.

When it was time to travel, he picked a direction and started walking. All forests end and so must this one. I wonder where I'll end up.

Reflected Magic

It was morning on an early spring day. The winter chill that still sometimes lingered in the air woke Conor early. The former knight of Scotia decided to make the most of the day and ride out to visit his godson.

Conor's godson also happened to be prince and heir to the Kingdom of Vilania in which his village lay, so Conor laid out his finer clothes. He ran a hand over his growth of beard and decided that today would be a good day to shave. Not that the king and queen would object if he arrived unshaven. Conor had known them when they were just simple farmers, and he was largely responsible for putting them on the throne. Still, they were the king and queen, and Conor would show them the respect they were due.

Conor walked over to his washstand and lathered his face. As he looked into his silvered mirror all thoughts of shaving fled when he realized that the face that looked back was not his own.

Conor had been trained as a soldier and had had much experience with the unexpected. Still, finding the face of a man of advanced years instead of one nearer to forty took him by surprise. He quickly took a step back, then recovered and stood his ground. Holding his razor in his right hand, he stole a glance toward the sword hanging over his bed. He wondered if he would have time to reach it if whoever or whatever it was came out of the mirror after him.

But the image of the old man remained in the mirror. It was a face somehow familiar to Conor. He thought maybe that it was his own, that a spell had aged him overnight. He ran his left hand over his cheek and felt only a three-day growth of beard, not the wrinkles shown in the mirror. It was not him in the mirror. The thought of a spell told Conor why he knew the face.

"Rasmus," he said to himself, and then aloud into the mirror, the second time speaking slowly and distinctly. He guessed that since the image had not spoken, he could neither hear from nor be heard by it.

In answer, the face in the mirror slowly nodded its head. Then it pointed to Conor, then to itself, then crooked its finger and moved it slowly in a "come here" sign.

This was not good. Rasmus had cause to hate Conor. He was the wizard whom Conor had once bested when trying to a baron's daughter a princess to her father. They met again in Faerie. That meeting cost Conor a year of his life. He had thought Rasmus dead. But wizards are harder than most to kill.

Again, Rasmus pointed to Conor, then to himself, and crooked his finger. Not wanting to break the mirror, Conor moved to turn its face to the wall. He would prepare to meet Rasmus on his terms, not the wizard's. He did not wish to be observed doing so.

As Conor reached for the mirror, the wizard did something so unexpected that it stopped Conor cold. For the third time, he crooked his finger, then brought his hand together as if in prayer. He was imploring Conor to come to him.

When Conor did not answer, Rasmus stopped his entreaty and instead held his hands open and apart, a sign from one knight to another that he was unarmed. Rasmus was telling him that he meant Conor no harm.

Conor took a step back from the mirror. He stood straight, then nodded his head in agreement. Rasmus gave a visible sigh of relief, then his face faded, only to be replaced by an image of a tower. Then the tower's image faded as well and was itself replaced by a sight Conor knew well. It was the castle of the king, the same one that Conor had planned to visit that day. The image started to move, showing Conor how to get from the castle to the wizard's tower. When the moving picture arrived back at the tower, it vanished. Conor was left looking at his own face once again.

The soap had dried on his cheeks, so he washed it off, relathered, and finished shaving. As he did so, he considered the journey he was about to take.

From what he had been shown, Rasmus lived a day's ride from the castle, on the other side of the kingdom. If he started out that day, Conor would arrive on the afternoon of the next. If he were riding into a trap, he would go prepared. He buckled on his sword and slung the bow which was a gift from Queen Anne of Vilania. He hid a dagger up his sleeve and put another in his boot. He'd make sure not to approach the tower at night, nor would he enter without certain assurances from Rasmus.

Or it could be that Rasmus did want peace between the two of them or needed something from him. After all, they had been living in the same kingdom for some time, and it was certain that the wizard had known where to find him. Yet he had not acted against Conor.

Conor saddled his horse Midnight and set off for the wizard's tower. On the way, he stopped at the castle. He saw his godchild and paid his respects to the king and queen. He also asked about the wizard who lived in the far castle and was told that he had been there for three years, and had given no one any cause for alarm.

It was mid-afternoon of the next day when Conor arrived at Rasmus's tower. The tower was taller than it had appeared in his mirror. It was built of stone, with no doors or windows visible. It was surrounded by a moat, easily twenty feet wide and who knew how deep. No river fed the moat, and no wind was blowing, yet its water churned and flowed counterclockwise around the tower. There was no bridge across. Conor rode around the tower but could find no way in.

Conor returned to the path that had led him to the tower.

"Rasmus," he said in a normal voice, as if the wizard was standing there before him. He was certain that he could be heard. "I've come as you requested. If you don't let me in, I'm going home and turning my mirror to the wall."

Watching the tower, Conor could see faint cracks appear at its base. The cracks formed a doorway, and then a door. Conor rode up to the edge of the moat just as it opened.

Rasmus the wizard stood in the doorway, dressed in fine robes. He bowed toward Conor.

"I bid you welcome, Conor of Tuam, son of Seamus, Knight of the Circle."

Conor recognized the ritual greeting and responded in kind.

"I thank you, he who is called Rasmus, who has lived long

and whose name and skills are known in many lands. I accept your welcome."

"Then enter freely and unafraid and depart in peace and unharmed."

As Rasmus finished speaking, a wind came clockwise around the tower. The water in the moat stopped flowing. The wind increased. The water grew solid.

"It is not ice," Rasmus reassured Conor, "And it will hold the weight of your horse."

Conor rode across.

There were stable facilities at the bottom of the tower. Conor saw to Midnight, then turned towards Rasmus. The wizard led him up the stairs.

At the top of the tower was the wizard's workroom. Conor was not surprised to see that from inside, there were five tall windows, each as big as a tall man, spaced so that Rasmus could view the entire countryside. That they also formed a protective pentagram was surely no coincidence.

In the center of the circular room were worktables, each of them cluttered with books, scrolls, and various magical instruments. Their tops were stained from the potions and elixirs Rasmus had brewed up. A full-length mirror, no doubt the one that Rasmus had used to summon him, stood on wheels along one part of the wall. Bookshelves, storage cabinets, and display cases lined the remainder, broken up only by the windows.

Rasmus stopped as close to the center of the room as he could, turned, and faced Conor.

"Conor of Tuam, twice before we have met. Each time we were opposed to each other. Now, let us be at peace. I swear by my rank as a mage of the fourth level that I bear you no ill will and will do no harm to you, now or ever."

This speech took Conor by surprise. By swearing on his rank, Rasmus had invested his magic into his oath. He could not now harm Conor in any way without losing much of his power. Conor could draw his sword to kill the wizard, and Rasmus would not be able to defend himself.

Instead, Conor responded in kind.

"He who is called Rasmus, I swear on my father's name, and by my honor as a Knight of the Circle, that there is peace between us. I will do you no harm, now or ever."

Just as Rasmus had taken a chance with his oath, so had Conor with his. For now and ever, while the two men may not be allies and friends, they could not be enemies. Should Rasmus later prove a danger to the kingdom, Conor could take no direct action against him. Still, if need be, there were others who could oppose Rasmus, and Conor could always advise them.

As soon as Rasmus finished with the ritual, his clothing changed from fine robes into more practical work clothes.

"There, it is done, and glad I am that it is behind us." He pointed Conor to a chair that the knight was sure had not been there before. Conor sat, as did the wizard.

"Perhaps, Rasmus, you could explain all this."

"Certainly, Conor, but first." Rasmus gestured, and drinks appeared on the table between them. As per custom, he let Conor select a cup, from which the wizard then drank. The knight took the other one.

"Must save on servants."

"A wizard should not have servants. Who knows what would be knocked over or opened? There are enough plagues and monsters out there now without more being loosed. And a good wizard does not need them." Rasmus ended with a smile.

"So I see. Nice trick with the mirror. I've not heard of that one."

"It is more than just a trick. Magic takes talent, concentration, and imagination. But you know that."

"Do you use mirrors to communicate with other wizards, or just to spy on them?"

"Mostly to spy. While I can send images, sounds will not travel."

"Why not just write what you have to say down, and hold it up to the mirror? That would have been easier than yesterday's pantomime."

Rasmus took a drink of wine before answering. "I tried that once. The writing came out backward. A mirror image, you know."

"You could use a silent language, like the signs the northern people use in battle."

"I could, if there was one that most people understood. But I did not call you here to discuss techniques."

"No, I gathered you need my help, or else you would not have summoned me or made peace between us."

"You bested me twice, Conor, and that is more than any man, mortal or mage, has managed. When I found that I had a problem I could not solve, I thought of you."

"What's the problem, Rasmus?"

The wizard hesitated before explaining "I have . . . I have been robbed."

"Where?"

The wizard waved his arms around, indicating the room. "Here," he said.

Conor was amazed. It was his week for surprises.

"A robbery, here?" he asked. Rasmus nodded. "From this room?" Another nod. "Someone took something of yours, something protected by magical spells, a tower with no outside entrance, and a twenty-foot moat in which are no doubt swimming all sorts of nasty creatures. Is that right?"

"As embarrassed as I am to admit, that is correct."

Conor did not see the difficulty of the problem. "It was another wizard," he said, as if that solved the problem.

Rasmus banged down his wine cup, not in anger, but in frustration. "Of course, it was another wizard. It had to have been. But who, and how?"

Conor took another sip of wine. His cup was almost empty. As he put it down, it refilled itself.

"You'd best tell me all about it."

"I began missing things about a month ago, a book here, a scroll there, lotions, powders, a skull. Not all at once, just something every other day or so." Rasmus gestured around him. "As you can see, I am not the neatest of people. None of my sort are. I thought at first these things were just misplaced, so I cleaned up, by hand, not magic, just to be certain. I found one or two things, but the majority were gone."

Conor leaned forward, interested in the story. Now that he

had seen the inside of the tower, he knew how he'd get in if he had to. A ladder across the moat, a rope and grapple to where he thought the window should be, and he'd be in. Getting in without Rasmus knowing it, that would be difficult. Getting in more than once, probably impossible.

"So it's an ongoing problem, a series of thefts?"

"Yes, and cleaning up only made the important things easier to find. I lost a valuable tome and a notebook with all my work in it."

Conor thought for a moment. Back in Scotia, when he was a member of the Ard Ri's Guard, they had had some thefts from the guest quarters. He had accompanied those appointed to investigate. He tried to remember what questions they had asked.

"Was anything disturbed that wasn't taken? Drawers opened, things moved, cabinets searched?"

"No," answered Rasmus, wondering if Conor had a purpose to his questions or was just asking them to be doing something.

Conor got up and looked around, He saw only two ways into the chamber, the windows and the door through which he and Rasmus had come.

"Rasmus, assuming someone could get through the main entrance or these windows, would you know about it?"

"Of course, they are guarded by my wizardry. Even if a stronger wizard could break the wards, I would feel the magic being used."

"What about someone who didn't use magic?"

"He would never get in, or rather, if he did get in, I would know it, then he would never get out."

Conor was still pacing, circling the room. An idea was forming. He walked over to the full-length mirror against one wall and stood with his back to it.

"Rasmus, show me where you kept the items that were taken."

The wizard looked around the room. "I am not sure where all of them were, but I think I can remember where I kept most of them." He wandered about the room. "The books I kept in the bookcases, of course, when they were not being used. If they were, they would be on these tables. The skull was here, and . . ."

Rasmus went through the room. He pointed out the former

location of at least a dozen objects that had been stolen. All the while, Conor stayed with his back against the mirror. Conor waited until Rasmus had finished before he spoke.

"Everything that was taken should have been reflected in this mirror. Someone is using your trick against you, Wizard. Spying out your secrets then stealing them."

"And how is he taking them from the room? Tell me that, Knight."

"Through the mirror."

Rasmus dismissed Conor's idea with a wave of his hand. "Impossible."

Conor smiled. "That's what I would have said last week if someone had suggested that my own mirror might reflect another's face. You yourself said that this mirror magic you practice took talent and imagination. Perhaps out there is a mage with just a bit more imagination and talent than you have. He's found a way to travel through one mirror to another and is using it to steal your treasures."

The wizard walked over to Conor, who stepped away from the mirror. Rasmus stood a while looking at his reflection before admitting, "I suppose it's possible. I do not see how it could be done, but that does not mean it is impossible. Before our first meeting, I would have thought it impossible for a mere knight to defeat a wizard of the fourth rank. A very long walk in a very dark wood changed my mind about that."

Rasmus turned away from the mirror. "No," he said, rejecting the idea. "There are wards on my mirror, to keep others from spying on me. I would have known."

"You say the wards keep other wizards from spying on you, correct?"

"Yes," said Rasmus, sitting down to take a long draught of wine.

"And that's how you cast the spell, to prevent spying?"

"Yes," the wizard was becoming irritated with this questioning and was beginning to prefer Conor as an opponent.

"Well, Rasmus, whoever he is, he's not spying on you, he's stealing from you. How can he spy on you when you're not in the room? The spell was incomplete. Your wards have no effect."

Rasmus was about to take another long drink when Conor's words caused his hand to stop midway between the table and his mouth. He slowly put the cup down and stared open-mouthed at the knight.

"Of course," he finally said, "That must be it. Well, I will put a stop to that."

Rasmus stood up and again walked over to the mirror. He began the gestures of a spell. Conor interrupted him before he had gone too far.

"That might keep him out and stop the thefts, but will it tell you who committed them?"

"Have you a better idea?"

"I might. Have you any powder, regular, not magical? Talc or something like that will do?"

Rasmus pointed to a cabinet next to the mirror. "There is some in there. What have you in mind?"

"Pick something worth stealing, something you won't miss if I'm wrong. Leave it on the table tonight. I'll scatter the talc on the floor. When our thief comes out of the mirror to take it, he'll leave his footprints in the talc."

Conor paused and looked at Rasmus as if to ask if the wizard understood. Rasmus indignantly nodded, and Conor continued.

"Will such footprints be enough for you to trace the thief?"

Rasmus thought a moment, working out the magic in his mind. "It should be enough. All that is required is some part of the object, or person—a piece of clothing, his image, something left behind. It is called sympathetic magic. A shoeprint left in powder is not the strongest of traces, but it should be enough for a wizard of my abilities."

"Then let's set our trap," said Conor as he started scattering powder over the floor. When the two finally left the chamber, the floor and tables were covered with it. The gold cups they had been drinking from were left on a table, bait for the trap.

Conor spent the night in the wizard's tower. The next morning, the two woke early, rushed to the upper chamber, and opened the door. The cups were gone, the powder on the floor undisturbed.

They stood in the doorway, looking at where the footprints

should have been. "Well," Rasmus said wryly, "It was a good idea. Do you have any more?" He started to enter. Conor stopped him.

"Wait, before you go in, let me make sure of one thing."

Conor carefully walked along the edge of the room, being careful to leave as few prints as possible. He approached the table from the side closest to the window and looked down at its surface. There he saw the outlines of the two cups in powder. He looked at the wizard, still standing in the doorway, awaiting permission to enter his own chamber.

"I thought maybe our friend had cast some sort of spell that caused us not to see his prints in the powder. You're right, Rasmus, we need a better idea. I'll help you clean this mess up while we think of one."

"Do not bother," said the disappointed wizard, "Just step outside with me and I'll . . ."

"Wait!"

Rasmus had started a magical gesture when Conor's shout stopped him.

"Rasmus, very carefully, step around to me. Come the same way I did, and do not step between the table and mirror."

Rasmus followed Conor's instructions to the point of stepping in the same prints the knight had made. After he stood next to Conor, he asked, "Now what?"

"Look in the mirror, tell me what you see."

"I see you, me, and a table that once had two very expensive cups on it."

"No, look down."

Rasmus lowered his eyes and looked at the reflected floor. Where in the room there was nothing but a powder-covered surface, in the mirror the floor bore footprints from the mirror's edge to the table and back again.

"But, how?" asked the wizard, who had once been very proud of his mirror magic. Now he felt like an apprentice, wondering how to do the simplest of magic.

"Let's think this through," said Conor, sitting at the table heedless of the powder. He pulled Rasmus down into the chair next to him. The two men looked into the mirror as Conor spoke.

"Rasmus, does your magic detect the trace of anyone besides ourselves having been in this room last night?"

The wizard closed his eyes, concentrated, then shook his head no.

"And the undisturbed powder shows that no one was. So the cups were removed by someone who was not in the room."

Rasmus started to object, but Conor held up his hand. "Yes, I know, it makes my head hurt just to think about it. But wait, yesterday you said that all that was needed to perform certain magics was an image of the object, correct?"

"Yes, that's correct."

"What if our thief uses his magic to see into this room? What he sees is a mirror image. He carefully enters the image his mirror creates of this chamber, rather than the chamber itself. That way, he cannot be detected by your magic, since he was not actually here. Then, while in this mirror image, he uses this 'sympathetic magic' you mentioned to steal the image of the object he wants. He leaves the mirror with the object in hand. It becomes as real as he is."

Rasmus finished Conor's reasoning. "And when its image disappears from the mirror, the item in my chambers ceases to be real, since it cannot be in two places at the same time. That is how it must be. But what about the footprints?"

"They were not a part of his spell," Conor explained. "They exist only in the mirror, since that's where he walked."

"So now what do we do?"

"You're the wizard. Counter the magic."

"I can think of one counter right now. Tonight, when this thief appears in the mirror, aim at the place in the room where he should be and shoot an arrow into his heart."

Conor considered Rasmus's suggestion. "That might work, but it won't get your property back."

"It will make me feel better."

"Not for long. Remember, I have twice killed you, more or less."

"You're right, my sort are very hard to kill, and even then, we almost always find our way back from the other side. What do you suggest?"

Conor was still looking at the mirror. He looked around the room, then finally turned to Rasmus. "You're going to like this," he said with a smile.

That night, Rasmus stood in the shadows of his chamber. He had placed himself so that he could see the very edge of what was reflected in the mirror. Dressed in black, he could not be seen. Conor hid behind the mirror.

An hour went by, then another. Finally, Rasmus saw movement in the mirror.

"Now," he said just loud enough for Conor to hear.

The knight quickly grabbed the sides of the mirror and turned it around. He rolled it toward the nearest window. Conor grabbed his bow and rushed out of the room and down the stairs, just behind Rasmus.

When the two men got outside, Rasmus conjured a light, and they searched the surface of the moat.

"There," pointed Conor, and they hurried over to where a figure bobbed in the water.

"You were right, Conor," admitted the wizard. "When the image in my mirror changed, so did the one in his. He went from standing in my chamber to standing outside it. When he fell past what his mirror could reflect, the pull of magic brought him here. And so he gets a swim in my moat."

The knight and wizard arrived at the edge of the moat nearest the bobbing figure. Conor drew his bow and addresses the thief.

"You're wet, you're cold, and you're confused. Not only that, but right now nasty things are beginning to nibble on you. I'm betting that you're too busy trying to keep your head above water to concentrate on magic. If you do not right now swear on your rank to return this wizard's property, and never bother him or me again, I'll loose this arrow and the fish will have a feast." Conor heard some mumbling, but it wasn't clear. He drew back further on his bow. Illuminated by Rasmus's magic, the swimmer could not help but see him.

"I can't hear you. Do you swear by your rank?"

A voice came from the moat. "I s-s-swear."

Conor looked at Rasmus. The wizard shook his head. Conor

spoke again. "Not good enough, say the words."

"I s-s-swear by my r-r-rank to all that you s-s-said."

Conor fired his arrow past the freezing thief. A rope was attached. "Grab the line, we'll pull you in."

By morning, the thief, a wizard who called himself Brandt, had made his peace with Rasmus and had arranged to return all that he had stolen from him. When Conor took his leave, the two wizards were sitting in the workroom, drinking wine, and discussing magical techniques, no different than two washerwomen trading recipes.

Conor left the tower with a purse heavy with gold and a quiver of arrows that Rasmus promised would fly true to their mark. Conor reminded himself that despite the peace between them, the wizard would bear watching. He would stop and warn the king about the wizard's magic and caution him to remove all mirrors from the palace's council chambers. What might happen next Conor couldn't say. It was, he thought with a grin, a matter for some serious reflection.

ONLY THE DEAD

The sound of thunder in the night. With the stars shining and no lighting in the distant sky, it could mean only one thing. Mounted men, an army coming from the west. One man ran to the church to alert the village while the others watched and waited.

It was a fair-sized village, almost but not quite a town. The number of men able to bear arms numbered about seventy. Half as many youths who were almost grown and who after this night would never be any older. A few old men with nothing left ahead of them but a lonely death.

Not enough to hold off an army, but maybe enough to slow it down. That would give the women and children a chance to escape to the east—half to the caves and the others to the coast with the hope that if the soldiers followed they would go after only one group.

Eight young men are chosen; it is not their night to die. Rather, they are to lead the mothers, wives, daughters, and young sons to possible safety and protect them as best they can. Those selected protest. They demand their right to stay and die. Inwardly, they are glad to be sent away.

The thunder is closer. There's little time. The evacuation begins as the defenders prepare to make their stand. Some hope to die quickly, others bravely, still others with bodies heaped around them. No one expects to see the dawn.

The army comes and brings with it the smell of death, the stench of decay. It is larger than expected and those on horseback break away to circle the town, to go after the fleeing villagers.

With despair in their hearts, knowing that all will be lost, the remaining villagers can think only of vengeance, of making the invaders pay in advance for what will be done to their loved ones. To kill as many as they can before death takes them.

They will be denied even that much comfort.

The invaders are on them now and can be seen clearly in the

moonlit sky. What has come from the west is not an army of men, but of the dead. Corpses march towards them, some limping, some shambling, some crawling but all of them moving steadily as if of one mind, one purpose.

A few of the men break and run. Though they will live with their moment of cowardice for the rest of their lives, they will get to live as men. As for the others …

The others quickly discover that the dead do not die again, that they cannot be killed. A pike through the chest does nothing; a sword thrust to the groin has no effect. Limbs may be cut off, but their loss only slows the undead, it does not stop them. Only decapitation works, but by the time they realize that a new horror is upon them.

As the villagers fight to clear themselves from futile battle, they begin to recognize their enemy. People from the next town over, and the one before that. The dead are men and women that they know from trading and fairs and festivals. They have feasted with these people in good times and shared with them in bad, rejoiced at weddings, and mourned at funerals. What has happened that they are dead and now attacking them?

The answer comes swiftly as the men of the village are overwhelmed. Some are killed outright, their bodies pulled apart and their dismembered limbs eagerly devoured. They are the lucky ones. The others, a mere quarter of the defenders, suffer grievous bites and wounds but are not killed. And as they watch the undead feast on their friends, brothers, and neighbors, as they wonder why they were chosen to live, they feel their senses begin to dull, their mental processes slow to where only appetite remains. And the last rational thought for many of them is a prayer for their loved ones—not that they escape, for they know that is nigh impossible, but that their mother, wives, daughters, and sons are among those killed and eaten, and not forced to join the army of the undead.

The army that devastated the village and which would go on to destroy several more started as one man, if "man" he still was. He had a name once—a name, a life, and a family. Then he lost it all and became something not alive yet not quite dead.

He, or rather his undead corpse, first appeared on the shores of the western ocean, that great expanse from which no one ever returned.

He woke up on the shores of a rocky beach, with no memory but pain. Pain from what should have been his death, pain of his revival, and pain from whatever or whoever had created him. When he awoke, he was afraid—and hungry.

He heard noises, and that part of his mind still working told him that where the noises were there was food, that the noises were food. Naked, he slowly rose and shambled toward the small fishing town where he would find his meal.

When the townsfolk tried to stop him he fought back with only weapons he had – hands, feet, and teeth—especially teeth. And soon he was no longer alone, as those bitten changed and joined him in his appetite and the need to satisfy his hunger. The number of the undead grew and soon the fishing town was no more. And those not devoured roamed east.

"How soon?"

Conor I, ruler of the kingdom of Vilania, turned to his most trusted advisor. "How soon before this kingdom is a wasteland like the others. How soon before my people become mindless, flesh-eating creatures?"

"A week, maybe a day more or one less, before the horde is at our borders, Sire."

Despite his worries, the young king smiled. "What's this 'Sire' business, Uncle Conor?"

"You're the king now, Godson, remember? Your parents went back to the farming they always missed and left you to rule."

"And in one week I'll be a king without a kingdom."

It was the older man's turn to smile. "I said that the horde would be at our borders in a week. I didn't say anything about what would happen then."

"So there's a chance?"

"There's always a chance," said the man after whom the young king was named, hoping that in his voice was the confidence he did not feel. The elder Conor was the man who put the previous king on the throne and who several times had fought to keep him there.

He had been a hero once, a knight who rescued maidens, fought giants, and slew monsters. He had almost married a lady and become a baron, but she had instead wed his most trusted friend and so he stopped being a hero. Taking what treasure he had left, he looked for a nice quiet land in which to spend his days.

It was not to be.

A couple from whom a child was stolen came to him and he could not deny them. He found the child and put its parents on the throne. A wizard who had been his enemy called him for help. Against his instincts, he aided the wizard and found a friend. And when the nobles of the kingdom suffered the loss of their jewels during the season of balls and festivals, it was he who found the slipper that led to both the thief and a bride for his godson.

And now it was time to be a hero again, to stop a human plague that left death in its wake and carried away worse than that. His king, his godson, the closest he'd ever had to his own child, was counting on him.

He only wished he knew what to do.

Reports of the undead had been coming in for months, telling of an army that could not be defeated. How do you stop things that kept coming regardless of the wounds you inflicted on them? Cut off their arms, they marched on anyway. Cut off their legs, they crawled toward you. Cutting off their heads was the only effective method, but for every creature thus destroyed two or more soldiers fell in battle and became the enemy.

This was not a war Conor could win, not with the weapons he had. They were only useful against mortal foes, not living corpses.

So where to find weapons to use against unnatural foes? Conor considered Fairie, that land of eternal youth in which he had once found himself. He knew the paths that could take him there. But time ran differently in Tir na nOg and one could lose a year in a week, as both he and the wizard Rasmus had had occasion to discover.

The wizard Rasmus! *Of course*, thought Conor and marveled that it had taken so long for him to think of going to his old friend and older enemy.

It was a day's ride to the windowless tower where the wizard dwelt, a day that Conor could hardly afford to spare, but what choice had he. Before setting out he called for the Captain of the King's Guard.

"You know the evil that is coming."

"I do, Lord Conor. My men and I are prepared to lay down our lives to stop it."

"Do not."

At the look of surprise on the captain's face, Conor explained. "These … things … cannot be stopped. To try will only damn you and your men to a horrible death or worse. Rather, if I am not back in five days, take the king and queen and flee to the Dark Forest. There look for a fairy ring. Once you find it, make an offering of blood and tears saying, 'A debt is owed to Conor of Tuam, Knight of the Circle. In his name we demand sanctuary.' A way will open. Take the king and queen through it and think of this world no more."

"And what of the king's subjects?" the captain asked. "He will want to see to their safety before his."

Conor shook his head. "You, the king, the queen, a handful of your men. Only these will The Folk accept. No more. If the king cannot accept this … do what you must, but see the boy safe."

A day's ride. It was always a day's ride. It mattered little if Conor rode fast or slow, or even if he walked, he would set out the morning of one day and as dawn broke on the next there would be the featureless tower that Rasmus called home.

The tower was built of stone, with no visible doors or windows. A moat surrounded it, twenty feet wide and who knew how deep. Deadly things lived in its waters, waters which no river fed. There was no bridge across.

As Conor approached a wind came up and the waters of the moat churned and flowed first one way then the other. He called out, "I call on he who is known as Rasmus, he who has lived long and whose name is feared in many lands. I, Conor of Scotia, who calls Rasmus friend and ally, request that he honor this friendship and grant me entry."

A door opened at the base of the tower. The wind blew again and the waters settled and became like ice. Knowing that he would not fall or drown, the knight rode his horse across and into the wizard's lair.

"Must we go through that every time I come to visit?" Conor complained once Midnight was stabled and he was enjoying a mug of wine in the tower's upper chamber.

The dark-robed Rasmus shrugged. "What is the point of being a wizard without ritual and mystery? Now, what brings you to my abode?"

Although not visible from the outside, the upper level of the wizard's tower was ringed with windows, each with a different view, not necessarily one of the surrounding countryside. Conor searched the scenes and found the one he needed.

"That does," he said and pointed to an undead army slowly on the move.

Rasmus glanced at the living corpses and returned to his wine. "A bad business that."

"They threaten the kingdom. What should I do?"

"Conor, my old friend, there is not much you can do. You can run very fast and in a direction away from that mob. Or you can hide and wait for them to pass and pray to your god that they do not come back. Or you could …"

The wizard paused and smoothed his beard, trying to think of a third option. Finally, he shook his head. "No, those are your only options. Run or hide."

"What about stopping them?"

"You cannot." As Conor was about to protest Rasmus held up his hand. "And before you ask, neither can I. Do you not think that since their appearance in the east those of my fraternity have not tried to put an end to these abominations? Whatever their magic, it is not of this world or time. It is a kind of alchemy that is yet to be, or so say the good witches of the North."

Conor shook his head in disbelief. This was not what he had traveled a day to hear. "Do you mean to tell me that no one in your brotherhood has ever raised the dead?"

Rasmus's eyes widened. He smiled and almost laughed. "Of course we have. To answer questions, to find treasure, to seek revenge, and to be honest, for some baser delights. A fine lot of wizards and magicians we would be if we never raised the dead. But never for long and never like this. Although …"

Rasmus's eyes closed as he brought up the memory.

"There was a man once, a man with skin much darker than mine, who claimed to have come from the land of the Afri, below that which we call Aegypt. He had with him servants that were both alive and dead. 'Zombies' he called them. The living dead."

"What became of him?" Conor hoped that this man was alive and close by. His hopes were dashed when Rasmus answered.

"Even wizards have standards, friend Conor. And some things cannot be tolerated. This Afriker was killed in the most horrible way we could devise. His servants we beheaded. We burned their bodies to ash and then burned the ashes."

"So there's nothing that can be done?" Conor asked dejectedly, preparing in his mind to return to his godson and see the boy safe before trying to rescue as many innocents as he could.

"Not in this world."

A light, a faint glimmer of hope in the darkness.

"And what of the next?"

"The next what?"

"The next world, Rasmus. You once told me of sympathetic magic, using the likeness of something to work magic against it. You just now told me that you could raise the dead. Let us do so and let the truly dead defend us against the living dead."

The upper chamber of the wizard's tower was silent for quite some time as Rasmus considered the knight's idea.

"There would be a great price," Rasmus finally said.

"For anything worthwhile, there always is," Conor replied. "I will pay anything short of my soul's damnation."

"Then it can be done."

The return journey took less than a day. He was in sight of the castle a few hours after leaving the wizard's tower. How this could be had never bothered Conor. The ways of magic were not for him. He merely accepted what was and went on from there.

Acceptance of what was and what had to be caused Conor to

travel far past the town and the castle that guarded it and closer to the edge of the Dark Forest. There he sought a dwelling of a different sort, a vast mausoleum in which the kingdom's past heroes, soldiers, and kings had been laid to their final rest.

Rather, what should have been their final rest.

As Rasmus had instructed, Conor waited until twilight to enter the great hall of the dead. Neither night nor day, the twilight time contained elements of both and so it was well suited for the living to call forth the dead.

"You can call the dead, my friend, but will they answer your summons?"

With the wizard's question foremost in his mind, Conor swallowed the potion he had been given.

"There is poison in it," Rasmus had explained, "poison and its antidote all in one draught. Not the correct antidote mind you, but one close enough to hold the final effect of the poison at bay. It will kill you and it will not and thus it will give you access to the gray lands. There you will find those you seek. The rest is up to you."

The potion burned going down and lit a fire in his stomach that no wine could ever quench. Conor's vision blurred then faded and he wondered briefly if Rasmus had been more foe than friend and had taken this opportunity for his final revenge. Then the knight knew nothing more.

Conor awoke on the cold marble of the mausoleum's floor. Looking up, he saw the tombs in which the men who had served nobly and sacrificed greatly were laid.

I've failed, he thought but then he heard,

"Who of the living walks among us dead?"

The knight's vision clouded over once more and when it cleared the great tomb was gone and replaced by a grand hall. Rows and rows of tables laden with the finest food and drink. But the men and, yes, a few women, who were seated for the feast were not eating and no one had a mug to their mouth. Rather, they were all staring at him.

In the center of the hall, at the head of what was obviously the main table, stood the man who had addressed him. By his manner and bearing he was, or had been, a king and Conor knew him from his portrait in the castle throne room. He was Roland, who had founded the kingdom and who had died defending it after ruling wisely for fifteen years.

"I ask again," Roland's voice boomed out, "who of the living dares disturb the dead?"

The living knight stepped forward.

"I am Conor of Tuam, son of Seamus, son of Liam, son of Conor. I am a Knight of the Circle, now in service pledged to Conor I, king of the land which you all once served."

"So?"

Roland's single word spoke volumes. In it was the disdain of royalty for all those beneath it. It implied that the one to whom it was directed was fortunate to be addressed by even a single syllable. And it was a challenge to make one's next utterance worthy of a king's ear or suffer a painful dismissal.

Having in his lifetime served and dealt with all sorts of kings and rulers, Conor was prepared and had his answer ready.

"I come from the waking world, from the kingdom which honors all those in this hall. I come in a time of great trial, a time which threatens to turn that kingdom into a wasteland barren of all life. I come seeking men who are not afraid to fight. I come seeking warriors, I come seeking heroes. Be there any in this hall?"

As he spoke these words Conor's eyes scanned the room, looking each man and woman in the eyes, his glance issuing the silent challenge that others may be worthy or brave enough, but are you?

The great hall erupted as Conor fell silent, the shade of each noble speaking up—calling for an explanation, threatening Conor, demanding satisfaction. Still others were proclaiming themselves ready to meet any challenge and wanted to know how and when.

A word from Roland quieted the hall.

"We are all heroes, Conor of Tuam, else we would not be here. But we have left the mortal world behind. Why should we now care what happens to it?"

"Because the threat comes not from the mortal world but from the dead, or rather the near-dead, the dead that will not die and will not allow others to do so. Soon the soldiers of our kingdom will meet an army of these living dead and many brave men will fall before it, but none will enter this hall. They will instead be forced to serve the enemy and will in turn destroy other brave men. Soon there will be no one but the dead, and who then will sing the songs and tell the stories that honor the brave and valiant?"

The hall was again silent, and Conor went on.

"The dead cannot die, not by mortal hand. Only the dead may kill the dead."

"Or so you hope." This from a woman in the corner, one wearing witch robes.

"Without this gathering," Conor replied, "there is no hope."

"And what is the risk?" A voice from the side called out.

"Risk? What hero talks of risk?" Conor countered. "But for those who must, if the dead may kill the dead, some of this number who dare leave this hall may not return. They may instead find themselves in a nether world where the dead go to die. Or worse, be forced to serve the undead. But they will not die a coward's death, for a coward would stay behind."

Again there were threats and challenges, but before Roland could silence them, Conor spoke for the last time.

"I will leave you now. I go to serve my king. I go to fight for Vilania. You may stay here in safety, eating and drinking and telling tales of past glory. But let those who are still warriors follow me and tonight we will write a new epic of bravery, one that will be told not only in this world but wherever men gather to sing the songs of great heroes."

Conor turned and, without looking back, strode from the hall and out into the night. And for a time he heard nothing behind him and was alone. But then came the clash of scabbards on armor, of footfalls on dry ground, of armed men on the move. Finally, Conor dared to turn.

And beheld an army, Roland standing at its head.

"The Great Hall stands empty, Sir Conor. Our swords are yours. Lead us to war and glory."

There were few to witness that final battle, when the Knights of the Honored Dead met the army of the undead. Some were shepherds awake with their flocks, a few were lovers meeting under the stars, still others were observers sent by the king's Captain of the Guard to keep watch and send warning of the creatures' approach. All said it was a sight both wonderful and horrible to watch.

It was midnight when the two armies clashed. The time that is between one day and the next, when the old has not yet given way to the new. Those who saw it, those brave few who dared to watch and did not run in fear, say that the undead were met by grey shades who did not hesitate but instead charged into their midst, swords drawn and lances and pikes at the ready.

And again these weapons had little effect. The undead things kept coming regardless of the wounds inflicted on them. Their arms cut off, they marched on. Their legs cut off their legs, they crawled forward. Cutting off their heads was still the only effective method.

But this time the creatures faced not mortal men but others like themselves. But unlike them, this foe was no untrained rabble but an army of warriors, warriors who could not be stopped save by weight of numbers, and for every brave soul that fell, there were two or three more that wielded the weapons that severed head from shoulders and caused the undead to fall.

Dawn came. As the sun rose to claim the new day's victory over the old, those who had dared to watch saw the shadows remaining on the field of battle slowly fade away, leaving behind only the headless bodies of those who should have been long dead.

And the word was brought to the castle, and the king himself rode out with his Captain of the Guard to find his friend and mentor. And find him he did, the one living man alone among the dead.

"Uncle Conor," was the cry as his royal namesake held him in his arms. "Guards, bring a healer, a litter, we must …"

"Don't bother, godson. The kingdom, is it safe? The … zombies, are they all dead?"

Not knowing what a zombie was, the young king looked around and saw nothing but the dead. And the dead did not move.

"We're safe, Uncle. And now we must …"

"No, there was a price, one which I willingly paid. Tell Rasmus that his potion lasted just long enough."

And with that, he was gone.

And when he awoke he was in a grand hall. Rows and rows of

tables laden with the finest food and drink. But the men and women who were seated for the feast were not eating and no one had a mug to their mouth. Rather, they were all staring at him.

And Conor of Tuam, Knight of the Circle, addressed those assembled,

"I come seeking warriors, I come seeking heroes. Be there any in this hall?"

And with a great shout, he was made welcome.

BIOGRAPHY

JOHN L. FRENCH is a retired crime scene supervisor with forty years' experience. He has seen more than his share of murders, shootings, and serious assaults. As a break from the realities of his job, he started writing science fiction, pulp, horror, fantasy, and, of course, crime fiction.

John's first story "Past Sins" was published in Hardboiled Magazine and was cited as one of the best Hardboiled stories of 1993. More crime fiction followed, appearing in Alfred Hitchcock's Mystery Magazine, the Fading Shadows magazines and in collections by Barnes and Noble. Association with writers like James Chambers and the late, great C.J. Henderson led him to try horror fiction and to a still growing fascination with zombies and other undead things. His first horror story "The Right Solution" appeared in Marietta Publishing's Lin Carter's Anton Zarnak. Other horror stories followed in anthologies such as The Dead Walk and Dark Furies, both published by Die Monster Die books. It was in Dark Furies that his character Bianca Jones made her literary debut in "21 Doors," a story based on an old Baltimore legend and a creepy game his daughter used to play with her friends.

John's first book was The Devil of Harbor City, a novel done in the old pulp style. Past Sins and Here There Be Monsters followed. John was also consulting editor for Chelsea House's Criminal Investigation series. His other books include The Assassins' Ball (written with Patrick Thomas), Souls on Fire, The Nightmare Strikes, Monsters Among Us, The Last Redhead, the Magic of Simon Tombs, The Santa Heist (written with Patrick Thomas), When the Moon Shines, and Mortal Sins. John is the editor of To Hell in a Fast Car, Mermaids 13, C. J. Henderson's Challenge of the Unknown, Camelot 13 (with Patrick Thomas), With Great Power ... (with Greg Schauer) and Devilish and Devine (with Danielle Ackley-McPhail).

You can find John on Facebook or you can email him at him at jfrenchfam@aol.com.

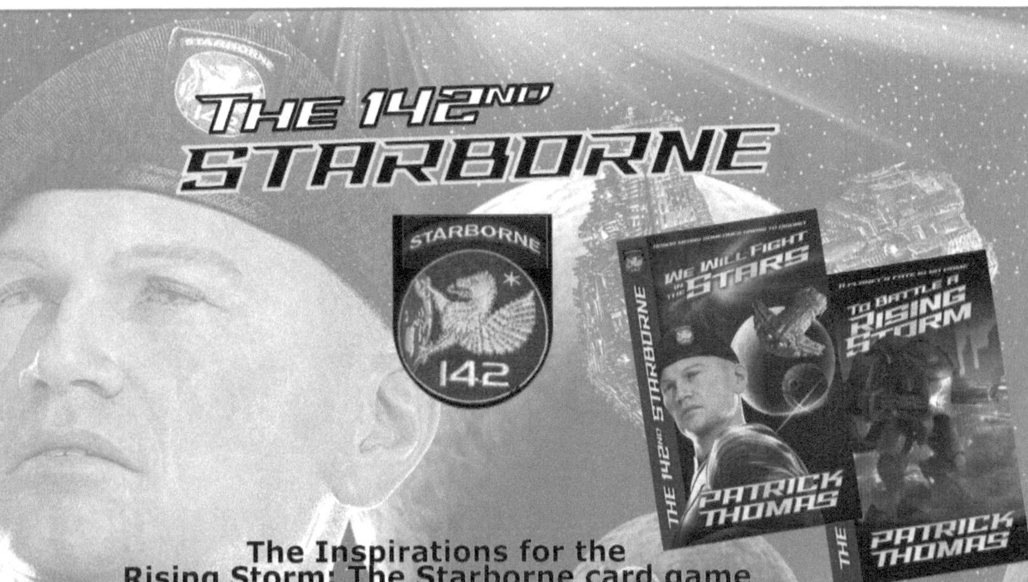

The Past, Present, and Future of the Abyss!

The Inspirations for the
Rising Storm: The Starborne card game

Welcome to the Freakshow!
Monsters Among Us
a Bianca Jones collection

PAST SINS

Bad Cop.
No Donut

THE GREY MONK
SOULS ON FIRE
JOHN L. FRENCH

THE NIGHTMARE STRIKES
JOHN L. FRENCH

Welcome to Baltimore!
Here There Be MONSTERS
a Bianca Jones collection
JOHN L. FRENCH

IT'S A CRIME
TO MISS THESE
GREAT STORIES!
from author
John L. French
WWW.PADWOLF.COM

APOCALYPSE 13

Camelot 13

LUCKY 13

You can't
get better
than 13!

DOWN THESE
MEANS STREETS
of Magic & Monsters walk the

MYSTIC INVESTIGATORS

Features all
6 books in the series in
one deluxe volume!

NO TEACHERS. NO PARENTS SCHOOL IS OUT.... OF THIS WORLD

www.talehaven.com

EVEN THE TEENAGE QUEEN OF DARKNESS NEEDS A FRIEND

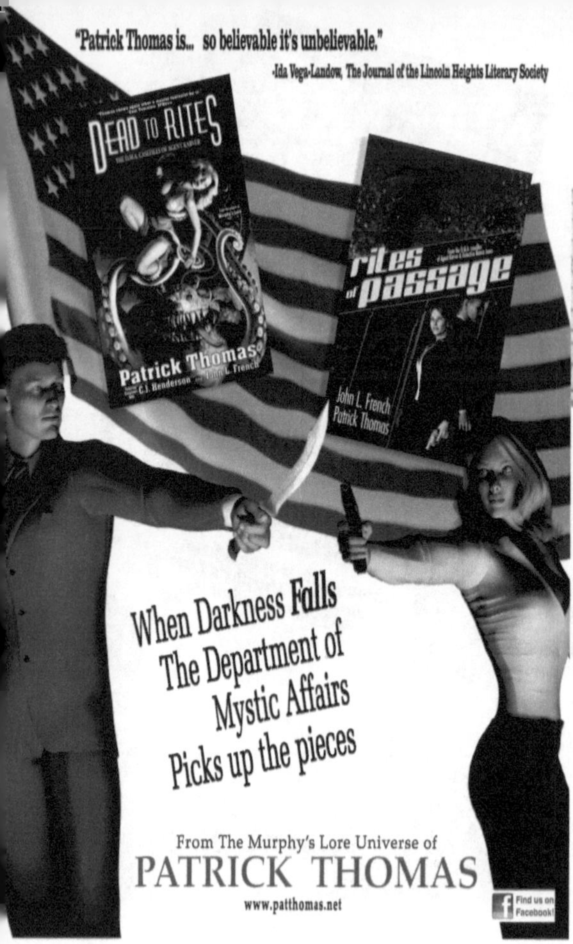

"Patrick Thomas is... so believable it's unbelievable."
-Ida Vega-Landow, The Journal of the Lincoln Heights Literary Society
Dead to Rites
Patrick Thomas
C.J. Henderson
John L. French
Rites of Passage
John L. French
Patrick Thomas
When Darkness Falls
The Department of
Mystic Affairs
Picks up the pieces
From The Murphy's Lore Universe of
PATRICK THOMAS
www.patthomas.net
Find us on Facebook!

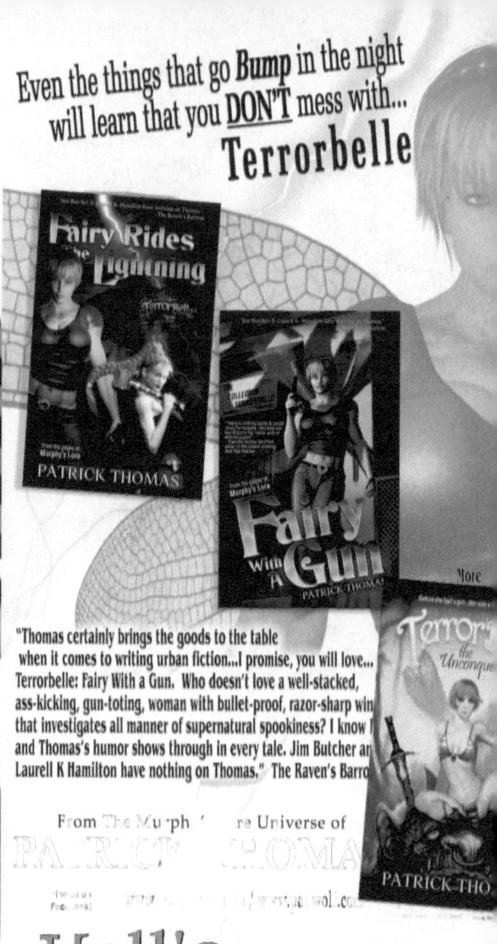

Even the things that go *Bump* in the night
will learn that you DON'T mess with...
Terrorbelle
Fairy Rides the Lightning
PATRICK THOMAS
Fairy With A Gun
PATRICK THOMAS
"Thomas certainly brings the goods to the table
when it comes to writing urban fiction...I promise, you will love...
Terrorbelle: Fairy With a Gun. Who doesn't love a well-stacked,
ass-kicking, gun-toting, woman with bullet-proof, razor-sharp win
that investigates all manner of supernatural spookiness? I know I
and Thomas's humor shows through in every tale. Jim Butcher an
Laurell K Hamilton have nothing on Thomas." The Raven's Barro
PATRICK THO

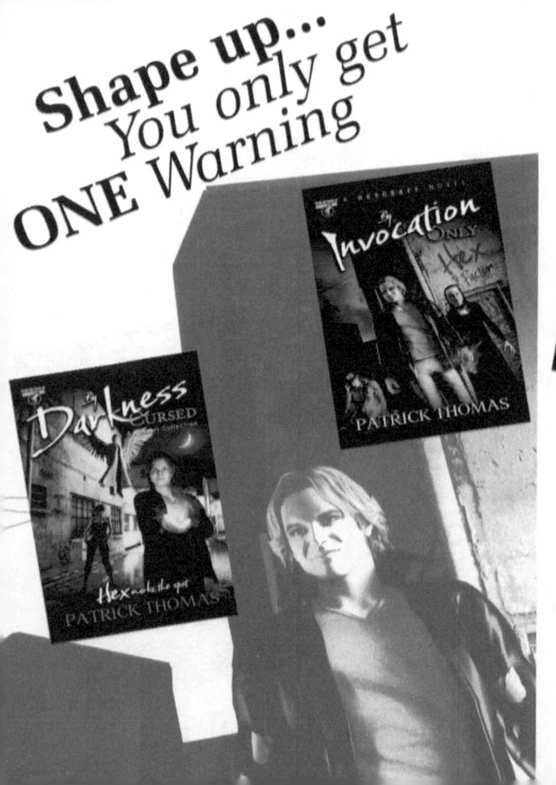

Shape up...
You only get
ONE Warning
By Invocation Only
PATRICK THOMAS
By Darkness Cursed
Hex marks the spot
PATRICK THOMAS

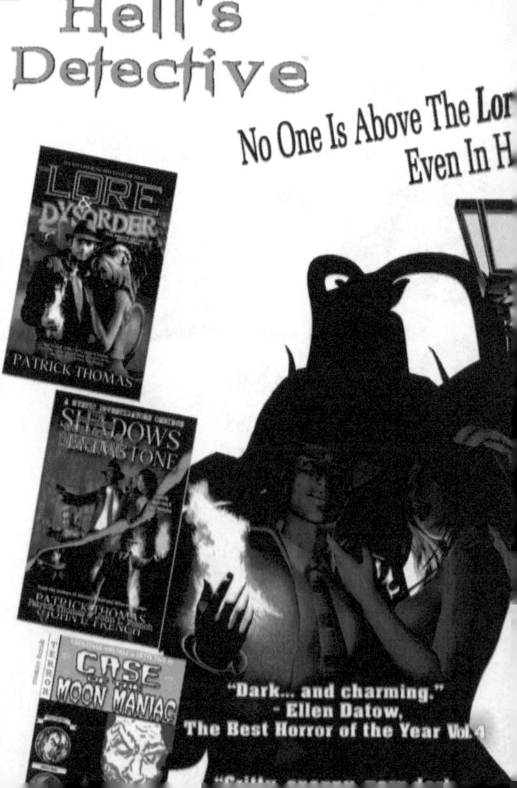

Hell's
Detective
No One Is Above The Lor
Even In H
Lore & Dysorder
PATRICK THOMAS
Shadows & Brimstone
PATRICK THOMAS
JOHN L. FRENCH
Case of the Moon Maniac
"Dark... and charming."
- Ellen Datow,
The Best Horror of the Year Vol.4

Help is only a Rainbow Away…

"Mix Gaiman's American Gods and Robinson's Callahan's Crosstime Saloon on Prachett's Discworld and you get an idea of Thomas' Murphy's Lore." -David Sherman, author of STARFIST and Demontech

"ENTERTAINING, INVENTIVE AND DELIGHTFULLY CREEPY." -JONATHAN MABERRY, New York Times and Bram Stoker Award Winning Author

"SLICK… ENTERTAINING." - Paul Di Filippo, ASIMOV'S

"HUMOR, OUTRAGEOUS ADVENTURES, & SOME CLEVER PLOT TWISTS." -Don D'Ammassa, SCIENCE FICTION CHRONICLE

PATRICK THOMAS

BIKINI JONES

**Being *CURSED* to wear a bikini
Won't stop this Hero
From *SAVING* the world**

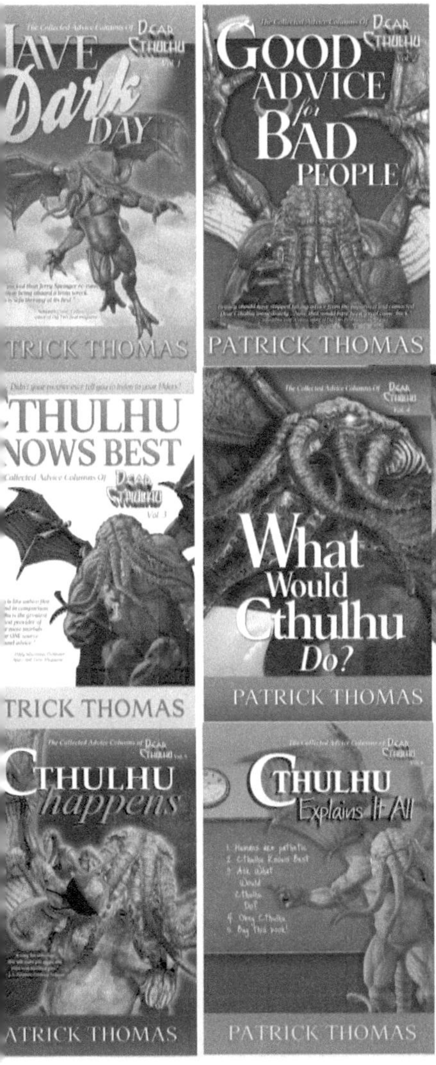

DEAR CTHULHU

**THE ADVICE
COLUMN TO
END ALL
ADVICE COLUMNS**

www.ingramcontent.com/pod-product-compliance
Lightning Source LLC
Chambersburg PA
CBHW020818190726
48285CB00006B/2325